THE DIRTIEST KILLER
OF THE YEAR was the man private

investigator Ed Rivers had to save from the chair.

Wally Tulman, Florida socialite, had been convicted of molesting and murdering a young girl.

Tulman's lovely wife begged Rivers to take his case —to prove him innocent.

Rivers wouldn't touch it with a ten-foot pole.

Then somebody tapped him over the head, just to make **sure.**

Ed Rivers got the message. Somebody didn't **want** him on the case.

So he waded into it — with both fists flying.

The Killer is Mine

Talmage Powell

PROLOGUE BOOKS

F+W Media, Inc.

Published in electronic format by
PROLOGUE BOOKS
an imprint of F+W Media, Inc.
10151 Carver Road
Blue Ash, Ohio 45242
www.prologuebooks.com

eISBN 10: 1-4405-3692-9
eISBN 13: 978-1-4405-3692-2
POD ISBN 10: 1-4405-5600-8
POD ISBN 13: 978-1-4405-5600-5

This is a work of fiction. Names, characters, corporations, institutions,
organizations, events, or locales in this novel are either the product of the author's
imagination or, if real, used fictitiously. The resemblance of any character to actual
persons (living or dead) is entirely coincidental.

This work has been previously published in print format by:
Pocket Books of Canada, Ltd.

CAST OF CHARACTERS

Page

Ed Rivers—A tough, knife-carrying private detective, he wouldn't try to get a rapist-murderer out of jail—until someone slugged him to make sure he wouldn't .. 2

Laura Tulman—Lovely dark-haired wife of the convicted man, she still believed in her husband's innocence 3

Wallace Tulman—Sentenced to die for the most gruesome of all crimes, he claimed he had loved murdered Ruthie Collins 18

Milt Collins—Ruthie's father, he swore that if the State didn't execute Wally Tulman, he'd do the job himself .. 27

Bryan Collins—Milt's precocious thirteen-year-old son, he accepted the death of his sister with disconcerting equanimity and told some telling tales out of school 28

Mrs. Madeleine Wherry—Ex-circus owner and hard-headed grandmother of the strange Collins brood, she fought Ed Rivers' every move to save Wally Tulman from the chair 35

Max the Giant—A hairless, earless monster, he looked like an elongated pink seal but he had the strength of a bear—and no-holds-barred loyalty to Mrs. Wherry 37

Evie Grove—Beautiful, doll-like, she plied the world's oldest trade and the world's oldest racket—but her race against time wasn't fast enough 38

Garcia—A dumb, sadistic cop, he should have contented himself with shaking down peddlers of pornographic art instead of tangling with Rivers 47

Page

Lieutenant Julian Patrick—He owned the Tampa police force, and someday he'd own the city. Meantime, he made a side career of frustrating Ed Rivers 49

Carrie Hofstetter—She lived off the fear of others, and could easily die in the same way. Giles Newell, her brother, was her sole support and chief danger 56

Stephanie Collins—Always a high-strung woman, the murder of her daughter drove her over the border line, put a knife in her hand 62

Giles Newell—The key witness at the Tulman trial, he broke Wally's alibi. Giles might still save the man in State Prison—if Rivers could find him 118

THE
KILLER
IS
MINE

CHAPTER

1

SHE WAS the kind who'd make the whole trip for a man, right to hell's front door.

Even a guy in his spot.

It took me a while to realize that. She'd called me twice. Each time I refused to see her.

As far as I was concerned the man in State's Prison at Raiford would get what was coming to him. He'd been found guilty in a court of law and justice, and I don't cotton to people who, without cause, kill other people. Especially children. Most especially little girls.

I thought I was through with Laura Tulman. She sounded like a nice person over the phone, and I admire loyalty. But twice-times-no should discourage anybody, and I dropped her and her doomed husband from my mind.

It had been a hot day, even for Tampa. The heat was a shimmering white wool shroud cloyed over the river, the shopping crowds on Franklin Street, the rancid tide flats along the Bayshore, the holes and hovels in Ybor City, the Latin Quarter. I have been down here going on sixteen years, but I never got used to the heat. I don't know why I didn't leave a long time ago. I just got here, got a job, and I stayed. That's all there is to it. So don't get critical. Why the hell don't you go looking for paradise instead of plodding through something you may be stuck with?

On the way to my apartment on the edge of Ybor City I stopped at a fly-specked market. The usual dusky kids were playing in the street and shrilling at each other in Spanish. The usual sharp, slicked-up characters were lounging around the corners, and at the domino club where the old men played for hours and the young ones devised plans involving women, money and women.

The usual smell of spice and pepper slapped me across the face when I walked in the store. I bought some Cuban sausage, eggs, half a dozen cans of cold beer.

I went up to my apartment in a creaking, gloomy old house and cooked my dinner over the gas plate. I was finishing off the sausage and eggs and the third beer when somebody rapped on the door. I grunted and got up to answer it.

A beautiful young woman was standing in the twilight of the hallway. She had tanned, smooth skin, great dark eyes and jet-black hair. There was character in the bold bones of her face. Her body was slender and her figure fine. She wore a white linen suit and carried a matching purse.

She looked up into a sweating face that's seen forty-three years of living. "Mr. Ed Rivers?"

"Yes."

"May I come in?"

"Sure."

She moved easily past my slope-shouldered, six-foot, hundred and ninety pounds.

I closed the door. She didn't belong here. She belonged on plush Davis Island, the man-made development pumped out of the guts of Tampa Bay.

She didn't turn up her nose when she glanced around. She simply looked the place over, at the day bed where I sweat like a hog when I sleep, at the second-hand TV set I watch sometimes, at the bookcase piled with old books and magazines and a few newspaper clippings that have come from being a cop of one kind or another nearly all my life. At the kitchenette where the remains of my dinner were still on the table.

She looked at me.

Slowly.

From my shoes. Up my baggy slacks. Across the sport shirt blackened and matted with sweat against my chest. To my face.

Her eyes rested there.

"You're not a very pretty man, Mr. Rivers," she said. "But I believe you are capable."

"Thanks."

"I have a considerable knowledge of you to bolster my opinion," she said. "You were once a city policeman in New Jersey. You came here about fifteen years ago, broken up by some kind of trouble up north. You just about went to the dogs for a while. Then you became a private agent for Nationwide Detective Agency. You've held down the job ever since. Your loyalty and basic honesty are legend."

"Thanks again," I said. She'd left out a few of the details. Even now I didn't like to remember the reason I'd drifted south. I'd had a girl up in Jersey City, where I was born and where I walked my first beat as a cop. I was in plain clothes when I met this girl. I thought she was mine, but she ran off with a punk I was trying to nail. Their car got in the way of a fast-moving freight train at a crossing.

I thumbnailed a drop of sweat off my face and said slowly, "I don't mind people checking on me, but you've wasted your time, Mrs. Tulman."

Laura Tulman didn't seem surprised that I'd recognized her. She was getting used to it. Her husband's hadn't been the only picture smeared all over the newspapers.

"Please give me a few moments, Mr. Rivers."

"I told you on the phone. I don't take this kind of case."

She tilted her head. In the dim light of the dying day, her

eyes were touched with loneliness and black fear. "You're very adept at saying no, Mr. Rivers."

"I only try to say what I mean."

I wished she'd leave. I also wished there was something I could do for her. Not her husband. Her. Seeing her, talking to her, I felt she had a quality rare among people. It was driving her. Causing her to fight a fight she couldn't win. And it might break her heart.

I drew my gaze from her. Just leave, I thought. So I can take a cold bath, relax, get rid of the weight of the .38 and knife for a while, tools of my trade. I wear the knife in a sheath at the back of my neck. Insurance. In fifteen years I've used the knife twice, and if I hadn't had it the first time I wouldn't have been around to need it the second.

"Were you at my husband's trial?" she asked.

I turned to face her again, shook my head.

"I don't fool around courts more than I have to."

"Then you don't know my husband."

"I read the papers."

"The papers crucified him."

"I've learned to read between newspaper lines. But there was a case against him. Strong enough to buy him a ticket to the chair."

She went white around the lips. "The papers and resultant public opinion ruled out any recommendation for mercy. The little girl's grandmother had a lot to do with that."

"The Wherry family is one of Tampa's oldest and most respected."

"So is mine, Mr. Rivers, but we tried to fight cleanly."

"That was a mistake. When your life's at stake there are no rules. Anything that cuts your chances is not clean. It's so stupid it's dirty."

"I know that now," she said. "But I thought our fight would be enough. He was convicted on circumstantial evidence, you know."

"That hasn't much to do with it. A lot of people don't understand circumstantial evidence. It's as good as any other kind if it determines that only one person could not have been innocent. If you've got any other evidence, take it to the cops."

"I haven't got it. I want to get it. I want you to get it."

"Let the cops get it."

"It's all over as far as the police are concerned. Closed. Like a book they don't want or intend to read any more."

"That's right," I said.

"But you could use methods they can't to get this evidence."

"I'm no back-alley thug, Mrs. Tulman."

"I'm sure of that, but you get results. I've looked into the records of every private detective in the state. You're the man I want. The man Wally needs."

"Wally needs to say his prayers," I said. "That's all Wally needs."

"You're cruel," she said softly.

"I'm trying to be kind. I'm trying to convince you that you might as well accept things as they are."

She looked at me for a long, steady minute. "Thank you for your time, Mr. Rivers."

She walked out of the apartment. I stood in the front room a little longer looking at the closed door.

Then I shook my head, walked into the kitchenette and opened a fresh beer. It didn't help much. The heat remained like a sticky veil of molasses.

I went to a movie that night because it was air-conditioned. Later, I went to a beanery and had a Cuban sandwich and iced coffee.

I walked home. It was late and the house was quiet. The vestibule was dark. The fifteen-watt bulb had burned out or the landlady had turned it off.

I heard the busy scraping of a rat against the baseboard. Then the rat dropped the roof on me. He hit me right on the bald spot. I grunted and went down. I didn't know it when my face hit the threadbare, gritty stair runner.

I was out only a few minutes. I was still in the dark vestibule when I came to. The whole thing had happened so quickly and quietly it hadn't disturbed the house.

A giant pain like a toothache filled my skull. It began pounding, with a rhythm so steady and dizzying that soured beer and sausage boiled in my throat.

I pulled myself around and sat on the bottom step with my head in my hands. If he'd still been here, he could have killed me. I was weak as a baby.

After a little time, I felt my pockets. He hadn't taken a thing. I didn't understand it. Ruling out robbery indicated revenge as a motive. There were characters who would have liked to see me pulped up good. But this boy hadn't beat me up. Just that one blow to show me he meant business and knew how to do business. Then he'd left.

I held the stair railing and made it to my feet. I dragged myself to the second floor and got inside my apartment. I turned on the light. The reception was terrible. Everything kept wavering in and out of focus.

I barely got to the old-fashioned bathroom with its gargling plumbing before the beer and sausage let go. After that, I stumbled into the bed-sitting room and fell on the day bed. I lay gasping. Finally I started hearing bells and realized the phone was ringing.

I twisted around on the bed and picked up the phone.

A whisper reached me. "Ed Rivers?"

"Yeah," I said.

"You're too smart to want trouble with the Mafia. So lay off the Tulman case. Tonight was just to show you we're serious."

The line went dead. I sat on the edge of the day bed, lowering the phone slowly.

The Mafia was strong in Tampa.

But this wasn't Mafia business.

The boy following up the vestibule job with a phone call had made one mistake.

I knew more about the Mafia than he did.

He'd known of Laura Tulman's visit. He'd figured I was on the case.

But he'd made a mistake.

I looked up the Tulman number in the phone book and dialed it.

Laura Tulman was home.

"This is Ed Rivers, Mrs. Tulman," I said. "You be in my office at two o'clock tomorrow afternoon."

"Does this mean—"

"It means that a free-swinging crumb came around here a little while ago and reopened your husband's case," I said.

CHAPTER

2

I SLEPT in spots and kept compresses on my head in the other spots the rest of the night.

Next morning I didn't feel like doing anything but staying flat on my back.

I got up, touching my head with my fingers. He hadn't broken the skin and most of the swelling was gone.

I went in the bathroom and ran the tub nearly to the brim with cold water. I soaked for half an hour, until the water felt as turgid as the rest of the climate. I dressed, boiled some eggs. I finished off the beer in the place and ate the eggs for breakfast.

At ten o'clock I was at the *Herald* Building going through stacks of clippings out of their morgue.

According to the paper, this is what the trial of Wally Tulman established:

Eleven-year-old Ruthie Collins had been molested and murdered early in the evening on April 15. Her knife-hacked body had been found in the patio of the home of Mr. and Mrs. Wallace Tulman, next-door neighbors of the Collins family in swank Brightwood Estates.

Ruthie's parents, Milt and Stephanie Collins, had been at a dinner party that evening. Ruthie and her thirteen-year-old brother, Bryan, had been in their home with their maternal grandmother, Mrs. Madeleine Wherry. Having given the children their dinner, Mrs. Wherry left them in the rumpus room to watch television.

At eight-thirty, Mrs. Wherry went into the rumpus room to announce bedtime.

Bryan was alone.

"Where is your sister," Mrs. Wherry asked.

"She went over to see Mr. Tulman," Bryan said.

Mrs. Wherry thought nothing of it. Wally Tulman had shown a great fondness for the child. She was often in his company.

At ten o'clock Ruthie had not returned. Mrs. Wherry went to the patio and looked across the lawns and hedges to the Tulman house. The Tulman house was dark.

Mrs. Wherry became worried. She had never wholly approved of Wally Tulman. She considered him "odd" in certain respects. For one thing, he went on periodic benders.

Mrs. Wherry went over to the Tulman house. She found the front door ajar. She went inside. She heard someone breathing heavily. It was Wally Tulman, sodden on a studio couch.

Mrs. Wherry turned on a small lamp.

She saw the knife first.

Then the blood in bright little stains on the legs of Wally's white flannel slacks.

She found her granddaughter sprawled just outside the glassed doors that opened from the back of the living room to the patio.

She called the police.

Wally Tulman claimed he had been drinking in the Brightwood Yacht Club bar until about nine-thirty. He had come home and stretched on the couch to wait for his wife's arrival from a Junior League meeting. He said he had been home only fifteen or twenty minutes when Mrs. Wherry found him.

The State produced a witness to prove that Wally was lying. The witness was a bartender at the Brightwood Yacht Club, Giles Newell, who said Wally had been drinking alone at a corner table. Wally had skipped dinner, drunk until about eight o'clock and left the bar. An hour and a half earlier than Wally claimed.

The medical examiner said Ruthie Collins had been killed about an hour before Mrs. Wherry found her.

In the face of the evidence, the jury didn't believe Wally's lame excuse. His earlier return, the knife, the bloodstains, ruled out any possibility of his innocence.

So the circumstantial evidence became more than conjectural probability. It determined a thing of certainty in the minds of the jurors.

Wally was convicted and sentenced to die for the double crime of rape and murder.

It was almost one o'clock when I finished sifting the newspaper clippings. The *Herald* had run enough copy on the story to fill a couple of books. It was prime material for sensational writers, and I've given you the gist of the facts that condemned Wallace Tulman.

He had got his comeuppance. Here was a young man with no visible means of support, married to a leading Tampa socialite. Here was a child, the daughter of rich and sophisticated parents, brutally murdered. Here was a colorful old woman, Mrs. Wherry, the widow of the late Spicola Wherry, who had built an empire of carnival shows, bearing up like a warrior, her hate for Wally Tulman filling a tense courtroom day after day.

Scene by scene the macabre plot unfolded for the papers. Stephanie Collins, Ruthie's mother, went into nervous collapse, tried to kill herself and was taken to a private mental hospital. Milt Collins, Ruthie's father, tried to drink a distillery into working nights and told reporters he'd take care of Tulman in his own way if the jury let him off.

It seemed the throwing of a high-tension electric switch was the only manner in which the tale could end.

I had lunch and went to my office to meet Laura Tulman. It was ten minutes of two.

The office is in an old building on Cass Street. There's a small room with a cracked leather couch and two matching chairs and a magazine rack and some magazines. There's a larger inner office with my desk, a couple of hard chairs, a filing cabinet, phone, typewriter table and beat-up Underwood.

The place was stifling. I opened the windows and turned on the electric fan. The noise and bustle of Tampa reached through the window. Traffic, and the hoot of a boat's horn on the Hillsborough River. And the faint, distant whine overhead of a B-47 from MacDill Field, a SAC base nestled close to Tampa. I wondered how the world looked to the boys up in the wild blue today.

She came to the office promptly at two o'clock. She was more beautiful today than she'd been last night. She was wearing a simple light print dress that made her dark coloring startling.

I pushed one of the hard chairs close to the desk, went around the desk and sat down.

With a half-smile, she said, "I presume you want me to sit down today."

"Please do."

She sat down.

I rocked back in my creaking swivel chair and said, "Last night I wanted your husband to die."

"Today you don't."

"Today I don't know. But today I have to be sure."

She studied my face. I've seen women feel afraid looking at my face. I've seen a few go hot and hungry inside.

This woman accepted my face.

"Will you tell me what happened after I left you last night, Mr. Rivers?"

"Somebody slugged me."

"Who?"

"I don't know."

"Where?"

"Late last night. I'd been out. It happened when I returned home. After he slugged me, he phoned and warned me off the Tulman case."

"But you hadn't taken it."

"He had no way of knowing that. He knew you'd been there. I guess he was watching you, knowing you still hadn't given up."

"Then you believe that Wally's innocent?"

"I don't know. I just have to find out, that's all."

"For Wally? For me?"

"No. For myself. I don't know why, exactly. I don't care. I don't analyze myself much. But being a cop is my business. I have to feel that I'm right for it. That I'm good at it. I guess any man feels that way about his job. It's up to me to find out one way or another before they throw the switch on your husband. I want to know who slugged me, and I want to pay him for that. I have to pay him. I wouldn't be any good for anybody around this town if people could slug me and get away with it."

I broke off. I realized she hadn't been breathing while I talked. Only watching me.

"Okay," I said. "That's that. And let's go on to something else. Sign this contract, please."

I shoved the printed form across the desk. She gave it a brief glance. "Seventy-five dollars a day and expenses."

"Whether I'm worth it or not. You have to sign the contract. I work for a big outfit. I have reports to make. Sign all three copies, please."

We got the detail out of the way.

"I suppose you want to know what kind of evidence I hope to find," she said.

"You've already told me."

"Have I?"

"Wally has convinced you the bartender, Giles Newell, was lying. There's not one other loophole in the entire picture. If the bartender was telling the truth, Wally's guilty as sin itself. If Wally was telling the truth, he might be innocent. In fact, he has to be innocent. There's no other angle you could attack."

"That's right, Mr. Rivers."

"And you want me to find this bartender and make him say what you want to hear."

"I want him to say the truth," she said.

"And if he's already told it?"

She closed her eyes. "Then God help Wally."

"You'd better tell me about Wally," I said. "And about yourself. The more I know about you the more help I might be. A pretty rotten picture was drawn of him at the trial. How much do you think is true?"

"A great deal of it," she said. "Just as the picture of you might not look well if only certain traits, incidents and factors were blown out of all proportion. There was some truth in what was said, but the picture wasn't true. Too much was left out."

"He drank."

"Yes. Sometimes. He was not much of a social drinker, but now and then pressures would build up and he'd blow off steam by getting drunk."

"What kind of pressures?"

"Simple human pressures, Mr. Rivers. Or perhaps they weren't entirely. Wally felt things more keenly than many people. He wanted the world to be a sweet and good and noble place. Such an attitude in our bruising world can make for pressure enough to topple some people."

"True," I agreed.

"But this wasn't the main pressure. That one came from me."

"From you?"

"Yes. I didn't realize for a long time. I didn't know. Wally was so quiet and agreeable that I thought everything I did met with his approval."

"Such as?"

"Stopping his work, for one thing. I didn't mean to do it. I didn't know I was doing it. To be truthful, I never thought about it—until it was too late. Wally was a magazine illustrator. A good one. But not so big he could be choosy about assignments. I didn't want to live in New York, so we lived here. The assignments gradually trickled to nothing.

"We didn't notice at first. We were building the house and Wally was decorating it. Then there was our social life, properties to be looked after here. This is my birthplace, my home. I wanted to stay here. I busied Wally with many things—and New York and magazines and editors became very remote things. I did it because I thought it was best. Perhaps I thought it was best because it was what I wanted and I was selfish.

"Wally never protested. He went along. I was the stronger. The more greedy, maybe. I think, now that I reflect, that he was afraid he might lose me. He had to choose. He chose me. But it did something to him."

"He miscalculated," I said. "He should have got tough with you."

"Maybe he should."

"You'd have liked it."

She looked at me calmly. "Maybe I would have."

"You were asking for it. He just couldn't see it. But that doesn't alter facts. Keep telling me about him."

"What do you want to hear?"

"Never mind what I want to hear. Just tell me about him. He'd miss his work."

"Yes."

"He'd get to feeling useless."

"Yes."

"He'd brood, maybe, and tell himself he was a kept man."

"Something like that."

"Then he'd go out and get drunk."

"Sometimes."

"How long have you lived next door to the Collinses?"

"About a year."

"You were close friends?"

"Let's say we were country-club friends."

"I don't have any country-club friends, Mrs. Tulman. You'll have to tell me what you mean."

"We were neighbors. Friends. But not close friends."

"You attended many of the same social functions?"

"A few. Are you sure this has some relation to Wally?"

"I'm wondering about his relations with the Collins family—and the little girl."

"They were not as pictured in court."

"We'll see. Did Milt Collins ever say anything about Wally's fondness for Ruthie?"

"No. There was nothing to say!"

"Wally was fond of the child."

"Of course. He doted on her—but he was not a monster!"

"All right, Mrs. Tulman."

"Quit using that tone on me! Why do you have such a knack for upsetting me?"

"You're going to get a lot more upset before this thing is finished," I said.

CHAPTER

3

UNDER my questioning, she said that Ruthie Collins had attached herself to Wally with the intensity of a lonely and affection-hungry child. The adulation of the little girl seemed to fill a need in Wally.

From Laura Tulman's overtones and expressions I gained a clearing picture of Wallace Tulman. A shy man. A man bewildered by the immensity of life. A man whose flesh wrapped frustrations, ambitions, dissatisfactions. A man adrift. A man reeling in darkness without the strength to drive a center post in his life. He had married strength and an animal courage in Laura Tulman, and he didn't know how to cope with these things.

The child had given him a purpose of sorts. In her eyes, he loomed large. He was warmth in an otherwise cold adult world. He listened to her problems gravely. He told wonderful old-fashioned stories peopled with elves and leprechauns. In these brief little worlds of fantasy both could find an escape.

But he was no monster.

There was never the slightest hesitancy, the smallest undercurrent of doubt in Laura Tulman's talk about her husband. The healthy animal vigor of her would have sensed such a thing. And if the little tentacles of her consciousness had ever touched monstrosity, she'd never have been able to hide it so well.

In a gentler world, Wally Tulman might have been an outstanding success. But the world was not the gentle place he needed. It was a place of atom bombs and wars and death and blood, and it viewed Wally Tulman with critical, bloody eyes. It held him in contempt, while in many ways he might have been more of a man than any individual sitting on his jury.

"What was Milt and Stephanie Collins' reaction to their daughter's attachment to Wally?" I asked.

"They never displayed a reaction, except to be glad that Wally would act as a sitter for them at times. Wally was always at his best trying to do little favors for people. Milt and Stephanie were glad enough to have someone watch after the child."

"Partying people?"

"Yes. Especially Stephanie. She partied like a person in blind, headlong flight. They had a great deal of money. Not only left by Stephanie's father. Milt accumulated money of his own. He came to Florida right after World War Two with a hunger for money. He got in on the ground floor. He rode the postwar boom to its crest. He was the man behind the Tierra Rose development in Sarasota, the Palma del Rio subdivision in St. Petersburg, the Crystal Tides on Miami Beach. Though he's only in his forties, he's a retired millionaire."

"Wherry money help him get started?"

"I don't know. Perhaps money from Stephanie's family figured. It was after their marriage that he really became a fabulous success."

"What was his attitude toward Wally?"

"Wally was never quite a man in Milt's eyes."

"That holds. How about Milt's children?"

"A by-product of his marriage. Little else."

"And a bother to Stephanie."

"Yes," Laura Tulman said. "She should never have had children. She harbored a lot of fears and anxieties. Her health was delicate, but she pushed herself to a frenzied limit."

"All right," I said. "You've given me a good picture of the background. Now let's get to the night the child was assaulted and murdered. What time did you get home from your meeting?"

"Right after they had taken Wally downtown. There was a policeman at the house. He said my husband was in trouble. He said he would take me downtown. I rode with him in a police car."

"Did you see Wally?"

"Not right away. A Lieutenant Julian Patrick was in charge of the case. He said some very cruel things."

"Patrick isn't a cruel man," I said. "Merely a cop without the smallest quality of mercy. It's all ambition with him."

"He didn't let me see Wally until early in the morning," Laura Tulman said.

"How did Wally look?"

"Dazed."

"Had they manhandled him?"

"Not physically. They had built a nightmare like a strait jacket and laced his spirit up in it. They had him so confused he half-believed he had really done it. Only one thing of importance was left to him right then . . . ."

"Yes, Mrs. Tulman?"

She touched her lips with her tongue. "That I wouldn't forsake him."

He was young, thirty or so. But his eyes had aged. He was slender. The bones in his face were finely cut. He was made for the part of a nice young host at a nice cocktail party.

He faced death with a childlike resignation.

A guard in blue uniform stood nearby as we talked with Wally Tulman through the steel-mesh screen.

"We've got to have faith in Mr. Rivers," Laura Tulman said.

Beyond the shadows of the screen, he looked at me and said politely, "I'm sure you're a good man, Mr. Rivers."

"Wally . . ." she said. "You've got to want him to help you."

"I do," he said tonelessly. He looked at her, and there was nothing much in his face. Then a shadow of sorrow, an inner weeping for something lost.

He put his hands against his temples. "I hate to think about it. I'd halfway got it out of my mind." He glanced over his shoulder toward a steel door. "There's a kind of peace back there, after the tumult of the courtroom. I had just about stopped thinking about it."

"You must think of it, Wally!" she said. "Mr. Rivers is going to save you."

"From what?" he asked without rancor. "I've thought of that. At first. The first few days I thought very much about it. Of some kind of miracle happening. I knew it wouldn't, really. But I thought of it, the doors opening, one of the fellows in a blue uniform telling me I was free to go."

He lowered his hands to his lap. "Free to go where? It would follow me. People would never be sure. I'd always be the man who'd raped and murdered a kid."

"No," she said. "People would forget in time. We could go away, if necessary. Or we could build a shield out of your innocence until people didn't remember any longer."

He looked at her and was sorry for her. "But I don't believe in the miracle any longer, Laura. I don't believe, that's all."

"I'm no miracle worker," I said, "but I know my business. I know how to work. I don't like to take pushing around. And somebody pushed me. Somebody don't want me working."

"And you think that indicates I'm innocent?" he asked.

"I don't know." I watched his eyes, the base of his nostrils, and the corners of his mouth. "Are you innocent?"

He sat looking at me for several seconds. His eyes held to mine steadily.

When he spoke at last, it was in a soft whisper. "I'm not sure."

"Wally!"

He glanced at his wife. "I'm sorry, Laura. I was very sure at first. I knew what time I left the bar that night. I was sick with myself. I started drinking that afternoon in a blaze of self-pity. I didn't recognize it as self-pity right away. I had to get blind drunk to see it. I had a horrible moment there in the bar alone. I smelled the whisky and tasted it and felt it roaring through me like a fire.

"And it was no good, I knew. The fault wasn't with you or Tampa or anything else outside of me. The fault was in myself—and I knew I was going home. Not to another bar, until I had made the rounds.

"So I went home. I had a good feeling when I let myself in. I was on the first edge of a binge, but I'd had the guts to come home. The urge to go, go, go until I'd burned myself out wasn't there any longer. I stretched on the couch, and the knowledge that I'd committed a conscious act of self-control gave me a strange kind of calm. I went to sleep, waiting for you."

He was quiet a moment, pinching the bridge of his nose between thumb and forefinger. "Next thing I knew Mrs. Wherry and the police were there. The old lady wanted to kill me. I could see it in her eyes, her every action. She'd never rest until I was dead.

"I didn't understand what had happened. Even after

they told me, I couldn't quite realize it. I loved the child, Mr. Rivers. She was lonely and sensitive. I loved her very much. I refused to believe she was dead.

"Then they showed her to me. Merciful God! They said I'd done it. What a sick, bestial creature this made me out!

"Of course it was simple. I hadn't done such a thing. I had come home too late to have done it. Then Newell said I'd left the bar earlier than I claimed. They thought I was trying to alibi my way out—after doing something like that."

His eyes became faraway, a faint glitter in them. "The policeman—Lieutenant Julian Patrick—always remained calm and so polite that it was a measure of his contempt. He stayed after me like a naked, unyielding knife blade. He wanted a confession. He explained, again and again, how it must have been. My mind had played a trick. I didn't want to admit what I had done. My mind wouldn't face such a thing squarely—it couldn't and still survive. So I honestly believed the lie my mind, in primitive self-defense, had made up.

"Yet it was all a lie. A lie. A trick of the mind. A defensive mechanism. I had come home earlier, desecrated and killed the child, and then my mind wouldn't believe it. It was far easier to believe that I had come home later.

"I fought him, Mr. Rivers. With all the strength I could summon. I lay in the jail cell telling myself he was wrong. I couldn't have done it.

"Yet—there were questions. Had I really been sure about the time? Why the strange inner calm as I'd gone to sleep on the couch? Because my mind had substituted a brief dream for a horror-filled reality? And why would Giles Newell lie?

"The questions got larger as the days passed. When I went into the courtroom, I carried them with me. Laura was sure I was innocent and would be acquitted. But I wasn't so sure—and if I had really done what they said, I didn't want to be acquitted.

"So you see, Mr. Rivers," he said without taking his eyes from my face, "I think I'm innocent. But I can't tell you with absolute certainty. I believe I came home when I said I did. I think I could never touch a hair on anybody's head, much less that of a child to whom I was attached. But Lieutenant Patrick's question remains. Maybe I am thinking and believing what I want to think, what I have to believe."

"And if the truth is in the question?" I asked.

"If the question reveals the real Wallace Tulman," Wally said, "he deserves to die. I would want him to die, because I couldn't live with him any longer."

CHAPTER
4

"DON'T TAKE everything Patrick said too seriously," I said. "In the first place he isn't a professional head shrinker. He's a cop. He's getting to be a big man in Tampa. He not only likes convictions, he has to get them to be what he wants to be. This case was made to order for him."

I glanced at my watch. The guard would be moving Wally Tulman back to his cell.

"How well did you know Giles Newell?" I asked.

"Not too well."

"What is too well?"

"Not as a friend. An acquaintance. A bartender. I always tried to treat him as a friend, but he didn't understand."

"He thought you were being condescending?"

"Yes—or afraid of him."

"Were you afraid of him?"

"No."

"There was no reason for you to be afraid of him?"

"No, other than his dislike of me."

"How did that happen?"

"Giles," Wally said, "disliked a lot of people. He wanted wealth and he disliked some who had it. Some he played up to. Some he simply fawned over. He didn't like me because I'd married wealth. That's what he wanted—to marry wealth. He's a very handsome heel, Mr. Rivers."

"You ever tell him so?"

"No, sir. I tried to be friendly because I've never liked the idea of having enemies. When I saw he misunderstood my actions I simply let him stay on his side of the bar and I stayed on mine."

"You never had words?"

"No."

"He didn't dislike you enough to lie your life away?"

"I'm sure it didn't reach that point with him."

"How well did your wife know him?"

Wally glanced at Laura. "No better than I did."

"He ever taxi her home when you were drunk?"

Laura looked at me quietly.

"No—and I don't like your insinuations, Mr. Rivers," Wally said gently.

"I'm not insinuating anything," I said. "I have to think of every possibility. If Giles Newell lied you into this spot, he had to have a reason."

"You won't find it in Laura," Wally Tulman said.

"Which leaves us at a dead end," I said.

Unless Giles Newell hadn't been lying.

But nobody said it, and the guard said time was up. Wally was taken back to his cell, and Laura and I went back to the world of open blue skies and beaming sun and free balmy air.

As I drove the rented car, Laura let her head rest against the back of the seat. Her hair lay on the upholstery, a sheen of polished ebony.

She was a beautiful woman, a damned beautiful woman. It didn't seem to have made her ugly inside, like a lot of beautiful women I'd known.

For my money, Wally Tulman had never been man enough for her.

Muggy night had crawled over Tampa when I let her out at her house. We'd eaten on the outskirts of Tampa. We hadn't talked much. She hadn't put the question a lot of women would have voiced.

She did now. "What did you think of him?"

"He appears to be a gentle, sweet kind of guy, the kind the world needs more of."

"But you're not sure."

"I'm sure of very little. I knew a kindly old lady once who poured kerosene over her bedridden husband and struck a match to him."

Her face was a pale cameo in the darkness.

"Monsters have some strange hiding places," I said. "I didn't see anything in Wally to make me think he's other than what he appears to be."

My hands were on the steering wheel. She reached out and laid her fingers on mine. "Thanks for being honest with me, Ed Rivers."

She got out of the car, and I watched her walk to the house. She disappeared in shadows. She had time to get a key out. Lights went on in the house and I saw her shadow pass a window.

I didn't start the car right away. From the window, I glanced over the neighborhood. I couldn't see much, but I knew what daylight would have showed me. The houses were sprawling, airy examples of modern architecture, built of steel, concrete and glass so that when you were inside you felt as though you were outside. Except that all of them would be air-conditioned. The roofs were flat and slanting, giving the appearance of dark, thin planes straining toward the sky.

Parallel to the broad, palm-lined parkway were broad, deep canals opening into Tampa Bay. Each house would have its private dock, cruisers bobbing at some, runabouts at others. There was no front or rear to these houses. A street level, a waterfront side. On the waterfront side were open patios and barbecue pits, tables and huge beach umbrellas and outdoor bars.

With a slight turn 'of my head, I could see the Collins house. It was almost a hundred yards away, most of it obscured by a high box hedge. You'd reason that you could never find a better place to bring up a little girl, a safer place.

I started the car, tooled it out of the driveway and ambled it down the street.

The Yacht Club bar was only a few blocks away. It snuggled discreetly behind a high, wrought-iron entry arch. Seaward was a quarter-mile-long row of boat slips where the bay had been dredged and a channel connected to the main channel to handle boats of any size. The landscaped grounds encompassed a nine-hole golf course and half a dozen tennis courts.

I parked the rented buggy on the circular driveway that reached around to the canopied entry to the club building. The heap was out of place, sandwiched between a Caddy and an Imperial.

I walked in. There was a small foyer, a dining room to my right. Beyond that, I guessed, were private club rooms where you could find a heavy sugar poker or gin game.

The bar was to my left. Its outer wall was a circular sweep of glass overlooking the water. This wall was lined with red leather booths. The bar curved out from the inner wall of the room and back again. A slim, jaded-looking guy was tinkling on a grand piano at the far end of the room. A couple strolled past him through the open glass doors to the terrace outside.

I went to the bar and sat down on a high leather stool. A short guy with olive skin and a small black mustache gave me a sidelong glance as he mixed a cocktail. He poured the cocktail into a glass and set it before a guy a few stools down from me.

He moved to me, raised his brows and inquired discreetly, "Are you looking for someone, sir?"

"I'll have a beer," I said.

He didn't move right away, and I looked directly at him and smiled.

He opened a beer and when he put it in front of me, I said, "Is Mr. Newell around?"

"Mr. Newell, sir?"

"Giles Newell."

The customer a few stools down the way lowered his cocktail, wiped his mouth with the back of his hand, and looked at me.

"Mr. Newell is no longer employed here," the bartender said.

"Since when?"

"I really couldn't say, sir." The bartender glanced at the man down the bar and moved away.

I swung around on the stool as the customer got up, killed his cocktail with one gulp and walked to me. More exactly, he floated down the bar until he was swaying beside my stool.

He was a big, blond, youngish, handsome man. His features were rough enough to keep him from being a pretty boy. He had a jut to his lower jaw like he was used to having people listen and do as he said. He had powerful, sloping shoulders, a flat gut and a look about him of golf, tennis and helming a yacht in a white-capped sea.

But he was a bird pulling his good looks and strength soft at the edges. His eyes were bloodshot. There were those first little broken veins in his cheeks and at the tip of his nose. The initial bit of flesh had sagged under his craggy chin.

"What do you want with Newell?" he slurred. He looked sore as hell. His eyes were dangerous.

I stayed on the stool, but I wasn't sitting the same way now.

"It's a business matter," I said.

"Well, find him someplace else," he said. "We don't allow bohunks and bums coming around here to talk to the help."

The bartender looked worried. He eased to the gate at the far end of the bar, lifted the gate and went through it. To get the manager, I guessed.

The guy in front of me put his hand on my arm. All the mugginess of the heat left me.

"Don't you know to speak when you're spoken to?" he asked.

"Take your hand off my arm," I said.

"I'll take my hand off when I'm damned good and ready," he said.

I relaxed. He was already so drunk he could hardly stay on his feet. His breath had that smell of an old drunk, a seriously built-up state three or four days in the manufacture. The final gulped cocktail brought color to his face and threatened to knock his pins from under him.

I turned back to the bar. The manager might know something of Newell.

The guy beside me pawed at my arm a second time. "You must be the lousy bastard she hired!" he said with sudden drunken clarity and certainty. "You're that damned detective, that's what," he added, running the words together. "But it won't get the bitch a thing! Newell isn't here and even if you found him, it wouldn't do you any good."

I looked at him and got a mental click. I'd seen his picture in the papers that reported the trial.

"How'd you know she'd retained me, Mr. Collins?"

Milt Collins glowered. "The whole damned neighborhood knows it. She made no bones about her intention to hire a lousy hoodlum to help get her husband off."

He weaved his face close to mine. He couldn't focus his eyes, but he tried. He meant to look mean and he managed to do so to some extent.

"Nobody's going to get that little creep out of the death house," Milt Collins said. "He's going to die up there for what he did to my kid—and to my wife."

His eyes clouded up.

He stumbled back from the bar. He stood in a swaying crouch with his hands knotted into fists. They looked like capable fists. Big fists of a man who'd once been a worker.

The bartender came back, bobbing behind a suave, dark man in a white dinner jacket.

The man in the dinner jacket had quick dark eyes. He smiled at Milt Collins and said good evening. As he did so, he stepped between Collins and me.

"I'm Mr. Ordway, the manager," he said. "I understand you're looking for Giles Newell."

"That's right."

"He no longer has a connection here. He left our employment right after the trial of Wallace Tulman. No one here knows where he went or presently might be. Is that clear?"

"Sounds clear," I said.

"We don't like our guests bothered," he said. "Nor our help. Please accept your drink on the house—and good evening."

"Thanks," I said.

Ordway relaxed.

"It's all right." I got off the stool. "You got a job. I guess you're okay at it. I'm not sore."

I started out of the bar. Milt Collins dropped a vile word softly and started after me. I kept moving. I heard Ordway say something with a brittle laugh in an attempt to get Collins in a conversation.

Collins' voice got a little higher. "I don't like Ybor City bums trying to get creeps out of jail."

I heard a stool turn over. I stopped then, and looked around.

As I did so, I bumped into a kid who was coming out of the foyer.

"I beg your pardon, sir," he said politely.

He was a slender, taut boy of about thirteen with fair skin, hair and eyes. He was dressed like a junior fashion plate and his hair was neatly combed. His wide, deep eyes rested on me for a moment. Then he continued into the bar.

Milt Collins was about a dozen feet from me when the boy paused before him. The child looked up like a little old man. "Father," he said, "will you come home with me?"

Milt Collins wiped his mouth with the back of his hand and stared at the kid. "Go home," he said.

"Yes, Father, if you will accompany me."

"You got no damned business here."

"Yes, Father."

"Please, Mr. Collins—" Ordway said, standing beside Milt.

"Go crawl back in your office," Collins told the club manager. Then to young Bryan, "Your granny send you here after me?"

"No, sir."

"You're lying, you creepy little punk."

"No, Father," Bryan said tonelessly.

Collins drew back his hand. His face twisted into a terrible mask.

The boy didn't flinch or try to defend himself.

Collins took a roundhouse slap at him before anybody could move. The swing was wild, and Collins kept on turning. Then he fell flat on the floor. He'd passed out cold.

Ordway looked at Collins with disgust. The boy looked calmly at the prone figure with nothing in his wide eyes.

A deadly little silence had come to the bar. Now there was a sudden buzz of strained talk and laughter from the red-leather booths. The jaded lad at the piano started tinkling again.

I moved to Collins and touched Ordway's arm.

"It's all right," I said. "I'll get him home."

Ordway jerked his angry face around to me. Then it dawned on him that I was relieving him of an irksome chore and responsibility.

"As you wish," Ordway said. "Juan will help you get him in your car."

"I don't need any help for that," I said.

I picked up Milt Collins and swung him across my shoulder. With the kid tagging at my heels, I walked out.

CHAPTER

5

IN THE BACK SEAT of the car, Milt Collins slobbered as he slept.

The little boy sat beside me in the front seat. He was as

aloof and calm as dead tropic air. He sat stiffly straight with his eyes directly ahead and his hands clasped in his lap.

"I'll direct you to our home, sir," he said.

"I know the way, son. You're Bryan, aren't you?"

"Yes, sir."

"Don't you want to know who I am?"

"I really don't feel it my business, sir."

"You mean you don't care."

"No, sir, I don't. I presume you're some friend of Father's."

"Not exactly. I'm a detective. Mrs. Tulman hired me."

I waited for him to say something. He didn't. Just sat there looking straight ahead.

"You know Mrs. Tulman, of course?"

"Yes, sir."

"And you knew Mr. Tulman?"

"It will do no good for you to try and pump me, sir."

I boomed a laugh. The kid had a cold-steel, nerveless kind of spunk.

"Okay, Bryan," I said. "Chalk one up for you. I guess I know when I run into a stone wall."

He looked at me then. Coolly. Carefully. I had the feeling he saw a lot more than most adults would have. "I didn't get your name."

"Ed Rivers," I said.

"You're a sinister-looking individual," he said.

"Am I?"

"Yes—as a sleepy-eyed bloodhound is sinister. I suppose you're a very good detective."

"I work at it."

"Most interesting. I suppose you meet many strange people."

"A few."

"And deal with all sorts of perverted ones."

"A few."

"I should like to hear something of your experiences sometime," he said. "Like my grandfather, I'm interested in unusual things. You've heard of my grandfather, of course."

"Sure, kid. Who in Tampa hasn't?"

"Mr. Spicola Wherry was the greatest collector of freaks of all time," he said. "He journeyed the world over to find them. They loved him. He said it was the freak, not the normal person, who saw and knew the world for what it was. At one time he had twenty-two carnival circuits in operation in North America and the freak shows were the greatest attractions. Did you know that?"

"I knew he made a boodle in show business."

"But the money never mattered much to him," Bryan said. "I've heard my granny say that. I went with Granny one Sunday to the town of freaks just south of Tampa. Have you ever been there?"

"Passed through it," I said.

"A marvelous place to visit. The mayor is a midget and the police chief is eight feet tall and the town clerk is a woman who was born with the skin and hair of an ape. I shall never forget how they came from their trailers and houses when they heard the grandson of Spicola Wherry was there. Many of them wept just at the mention of Grandfather's name."

We were close to the Collins house.

"Of course," Bryan said, his tone holding its recent spark of animation, "the greatest freak of all time is Max the Giant. Have you ever seen him?"

"I don't think so."

"He watches after Granny. When Grandfather died, Max was his valet and servant. I can remember what Max did after the funeral. I was a small boy then, but I remember clearly. I was peeking through a doorway. I'd started in to see Granny, and I saw Max kneeling down before her. He said his only wish was to carry on in the service of Grandfather's ghost and Grandfather's widow."

"Must be quite a guy."

"Most fearsome to some people, but only because they're narrow and lack understanding. He was born without a single hair on him. None on his head. No eyebrows. His skin is shiny, like pink silk. He stands nearly seven feet tall and fills up a doorway. He used to perform great feats of strength in Grandfather's shows. He challenged all comers among the local rubes in wrestling matches, with a thousand dollars in prize money if the rube could pin him in thirty minutes. In his entire career, he never cost Grandfather the thousand."

"Quite a man."

"He is, indeed! If he had ears, people might accept him more readily."

"He's got no ears?"

"None at all. He was born that way. Grandfather found him on a barren New England farm. I've heard the story many times. Max the Giant was like a wild creature of the woods. It came from having the normal ones torment him. It took Grandfather quite a long time to win him over. Now Max doesn't have anybody joke about his ears. He's far too big for that. In fact, he joked himself about it once. To me. He said, 'People always talking about needing this or that like they need a hole in the head. Lucky for old Max he was born with two holes in the head, eh, little Wherry?' "

"Then he isn't deaf?"

"Of course not. He hears better than most people, sounds aft as well as fore," Bryan said. "I think his joke was quite clever."

I swung into the driveway and stopped the car under the port attached to the dark house.

Bryan opened the door on his side. "I'll go in and turn on some lights for you."

He got out, went around the car and marched sturdily into the house. A few seconds later, lights went on inside.

I got out, opened the rear door of the car, grunted Milt Collins' form over my shoulder. He struggled a little and cursed thickly as I carried him into the house.

Bryan led me to a bedroom and held the door open. "You may put him there."

I dropped Milt Collins across the bed. He cursed some more. I went out, and Bryan closed the door on his father's cursing, which gradually dribbled down to nothing.

Bryan dusted his hands and we walked back to the living area of the house. The place was sprawling and spacious, richly furnished. The use of glass and indoor planters, lushly green, seemed to bring the whole of the outdoors into the house. It was a place made for bountiful living.

Bryan seated himself in a big, square chair and rested his hands on its arms. "I suppose Father will be quite ill when he wakes."

"You're by yourself here?"

"For the moment. Our house servant quit this afternoon. We've had a succession of them since Ruthie was killed and my mother went to the insane asylum."

"I see. Maybe I better stick around."

"You're welcome to stay or go, sir. You needn't stay on my account. I have plenty of books and the television. And Granny will drop over, I suppose. I phoned to see if Father was there to tell him about the servant quitting."

"Sure you won't be lonely?"

"Lonely?" he echoed, as if the word was strange. "No, I think not." He regarded me dispassionately. "I suppose you're thinking about Ruthie and my mother?"

"Well, I—"

"It's quite all right, sir. What is done is done, as Grandfather would say, and you can't undo it, can you?" His wide, bland eyes rested on mine.

"I guess you can't," I said.

"Were the facts altered, things might be worse. Ruthie was the lonely one. Rather like Mother. Frantic, from loneliness. It made for mischief sometimes. Like the time when Ruthie took the fish bowl—"

"Son, if you don't want to confide in a stranger, you sure don't have to."

"You're a detective. You came to ask questions, didn't you?"

"Not to pick kids," I said.

"You tried to pump me about Mr. and Mrs. Tulman."

"Not exactly."

"Well, really, I don't mind answering questions. I realize what you're trying to do. You'd like to know about Ruthie. And Mother and Father. And Mr. and Mrs. Tulman. There's little to know, really, that didn't come out at the trial. Ruthie's mischief came from wishing she was like poor children, who could run as they pleased and have playmates. It hurt her to be bad and she was bad sometimes so she could feel loneliness was about all she deserved. The time she put household ammonia in the fish bowl, she wasn't mad at the fish. They just didn't matter—until they curled up and died. Then Ruthie wept."

"Any kid's liable to pull a few stunts like that in growing up," I said. "Hardly a kid living that didn't sometime pull the wings off a fly or pour salt on a snail or pop a bird or two with his first BB gun."

"Perhaps you're right, sir."

A car drove up and stopped outside.

"I wouldn't be at all surprised if that's Granny," Bryan said, getting out of his chair.

The glass doors slapped open and an old lady came in with all the grace of a free-wheeling boxcar. She was dressed in black and it made her rough-featured, densely powdered face look chalky. She had her steel-gray hair piled in a bun on top of her head. The bun was held with rhinestone pins and she dripped more rhinestones from her creased neck, ears and fingers.

She laid her hand on Bryan's shoulder. "Find your father?"

"Yes, Grandmère."

Mrs. Madeleine Wherry turned her attention to me. "Who're you?"

"The name is Ed Rivers," I said.

"He's the detective Mrs. Tulman hired," Bryan said.

The hefty old lady took a few slow steps toward me. Her eyes reminded me of a snapping turtle's when the turtle is about to break the back of a fish.

"Mr. Rivers," she said quietly, "the Tulman affair was settled quite legally and honestly in court."

"I'm a working man, Mrs. Wherry. I have to make a living."

"Is that all you're doing? Taking a client's fee for the mere sake of living, even knowing the man's guilty and beyond help?"

"I try to give an honest day's work for an honest dollar," I said.

She stood sizing me up. Her eyes were cold and wise. She was trying to decide whether I was a shyster type or the kind to take a fee seriously.

"Mr. Rivers," she said at last, "you're facing certain failure."

"You may be right, Mrs. Wherry."

"Damn you," she said calmly, "don't use that patronizing tone on me. There isn't a chance of Wally Tulman being innocent."

"I don't blame you for hating him."

"Hating him?" she said softly. "Raw hate is love compared to what I feel for that monster! Almost equally, I despise his wife. It was she who brought him into our world, our lives. Perhaps you haven't fully thought about what Wallace Tulman did to me and mine, Mr. Rivers."

"I have."

"No, you haven't—or you'd want that man to die, as he deserves. He killed a child. He destroyed the child's mother, my daughter. He made wreckage out of the life of my son-in-law." She gave a little gasp. "They're all I have in this world, Mr. Rivers."

"I'm quite sympathetic."

"Then seek your living someplace else. If it's a matter of money, I'm not a stingy person."

"I don't buy off very easy, Mrs. Wherry."

"I could meet your price."

"The price of hiding something?"

Color grew in purple blotches on the loose, heavy skin of her cheeks. It showed like bruises beneath the face powder. "Mr. Rivers, I don't believe I made myself clear. We have nothing to hide. Nothing whatever. The newspapers have made capital of us. None of us can take much more. I have never bent my neck to anything in this life, but my neck is growing tired. My son-in-law must be left alone if he is to find his way back to some semblance of sobriety. And my grandson"—she put her arm across Bryan's shoulders and drew him close to her—"must not be scarred beyond repair. Now can you understand that? All our dirty linen, our weaknesses, our privacy, have been bared to public view. The man responsible will die in the electric chair —after the damage is done. We simply can't afford more damage. What would it accomplish? How could it help anyone?"

She stopped speaking, a glistening of spittle on her rouged lips. "You stand ashamed, Mr. Rivers."

"No," I said, "I'm not ashamed. I'm sorry for you."

"We're grateful for that," she said shortly. "I hope you're sorry enough to understand and not torment us. If you'd name a price—"

"I don't have a price, Mrs. Wherry. I wish sometimes I did. It would make life simpler."

"You beast!" she said simply.

Bryan looked up at her face. "He brought Father home, Grandmère."

"For that I'll pay you, Mr. Rivers."

"There's no charge," I said.

"He questioned me, Granny," Bryan said.

She looked at me and said, "I see I flattered you. I apologize to the kingdom of beasts. You're really a snake. Now get out of here!"

I turned to go.

I hadn't seen or heard him come in, but Max the Giant was standing near the outside doors. He was as big as Bryan had said. The only excess weight he carried was the weight of his clothes. He had a hickory neck growing out of his shoulders that curved to form a pink silk seal's head.

He looked past me at Mrs. Wherry hungrily. He failed to give him a signal and the eyes in the pale seal's head showed disappointment.

I walked out of the room.

CHAPTER

6

WHEN I got to my apartment and opened the door I smelled fresh cigarette smoke. I put my hand on the .38 and used my other hand to turn on a light.

She sat up on the day bed. She was a good-looking young animal, tallish and sleek. Her print dress flowed against the vigor of her thighs, hips and bosom. She had bedroom blond hair framing a face that was almost pretty as a doll's. The lips were a little lush for a doll's.

She pushed back her blond hair where it had fallen across the side of her forehead.

"Hello," she said. "What took you so long?"

"This and that."

"Got a cigarette?"

I walked across the room and handed her a cigarette. She put it between her ripe cherry lips and waited for me to light it. I struck a match from a paper book. As she leaned forward to accept the light, I said, "Who the hell are you?"

"Evie Grove."

"Never heard of you."

"I know you haven't. But I've heard of you, Ed. You're looking for Giles Newell."

"Word does get around. How'd you get in here?"

"Oh, it's an old-fashioned lock. A lousy lock."

"Giles Newell a friend of yours?"

"Could be," she said, taking a deep puff from the cigarette.

"What else could he be?"

She shrugged. "Business acquaintance."

"Help you pay the rent?"

"Ummmm."

"I see," I said. "How has the hostess business been?"

"I can't complain. That is, I couldn't—as long as Giles was working at the Yacht Club. I have a comfortable cottage nearby. There was always a yachting party making up that needed an extra girl, or some poor guy out on the town without companionship."

I've walked down the dirty side of life for a long time, but I still feel a little sad pang when I cross an Evie. All that beauty put into the shallow, dead-end service of whore-dom. She'd get only a few years of luxury at best. There was too much competition, too much beauty of the flesh that hated the idea of slinging hash or working in a cigar factory.

"So Giles took off," I said, "and your phone hasn't been ringing."

"My rent's overdue," she admitted.

"And Ordway won't have you working the club on your own."

"Something like that. I guess he does have to think of appearances. Still, the little priss could give me a break. I've steered a lot of drinking business his way."

I went into the kitchenette to make some ice water.

"Aren't you going to ask me where Giles is?" she called after me.

"If you knew, you wouldn't be here."

"That's right," she said with a laugh. She had a damned fine laugh, musical and carefree. Maybe she'd practiced a long time to work up that laugh. It was a tool of her trade.

I came to her carrying two glasses of ice water. I handed her one. She sipped it and made a face.

"It won't poison you," I said.

"Are you sure?" she laughed again. "Since it's you telling me, I'll take a chance." She drank the water, set the glass on the floor beside the day bed, and leaned back. She half-reclined against her elbows. The print dress sighed against her firm flesh as she moved.

"You know," she said, "I believe you'll find Giles."

"Maybe."

"I believe you could do about anything you wanted to. You're not at all like Giles."

"No?"

She gave a vague wave with her hand. "He was good looking—and you don't look so good. He was a sleek physical specimen and kept himself in the best of shape—and you look sleepy and tired and sloppy. He would get on his knees and crawl if it would give him an in with somebody of wealth—and I guess you'd spit on somebody, wealthy or not, if you thought he deserved spitting on."

"I don't know," I said. "I just try to mind my own business. I find it's better that way."

"Oh, Giles minded his own business, all right. He was on the make for a rich one. Young, old, hag or bag, he didn't care. Just so long as she was wealthy. He would get so frustrated sometimes, seeing all that wealth and having none of it, that tears would come to his eyes."

"I guess he didn't like Wallace Tulman very well."

"I saw him at the trial. Giles, I mean. It made him writhe inside that bumbling, namby-pamby Tulman had married money when Giles, handsome and smooth, couldn't seem to make a right connection."

"You're talking about Giles in the past tense."

"So?"

"So does it mean anything?"

"Such as?"

"You sound as if he's dead. The way you describe him and all."

She dropped her head back and began laughing in earnest. The curve of her throat was slim and vibrant. Then she sat up. "Maybe the dirty son is dead. I wouldn't know. I haven't seen him since he took off. Do you always try to read so much into so little?"

"I guess I do. Once in a while I'm right."

"And rough about it."

"Not intentionally."

She turned her head and looked at me out of the corners of her eyes. "Leave Giles in one piece when you locate him, will you?"

"For you?"

"My rent's overdue, remember? Giles must have figured the scandal and messiness of the trial had fouled him up here. When you find him, he'll be working in some swank spot, still looking for that hen with the golden eggs. I need a connection in a swank spot, Ed Rivers."

She rose slowly to her feet. "Of course, I might find Giles first."

"Maybe."

"So I wouldn't try to help him hide. I'd want to feel free to call you."

"Why?"

"Because, silly, it would be the best way. You'll keep on hunting him. If I find him first, why not arrange it so you can talk to him and get it over with."

"You're not worried about what he might say to me?"

She smiled, showing a little of her even white teeth. "What could he say? I think he told the truth at the trial. He despised Wallace Tulman—but not that much. Anyhow, if he'd wanted to lie, wouldn't it have been better for him to lie Wally out of it?"

"For money?"

She shrugged. "What else?"

"How much do you want if you find Giles before I do?"

"Five thousand dollars."

"Pretty high payment."

"Please, Ed. I never take payment for anything. Just a favor in return for a favor."

"It's still too much," I said.

"Four thousand?"

"Be reasonable."

"Don't be a piker," she said, almost gaily. "It wouldn't be your money. Think of the time and effort I might save you."

"A thousand dollars," I said. "Provided I can get Mrs. Tulman to agree."

"That the best I can do?"

· "Take it or leave it," I said.

"Okay. Every little bit helps."

"That's right. You have a pretty good idea where Giles is, don't you?"

She shook her head.

"Now you're telling a little white one," I said. "You figure I'll get to him, and you figure further to get your lump in before it's too late and pick up an easy thousand dollars."

She smiled and rubbed my cheek with the back of her hand. "What a suspicious barbarian you are!"

"Where is he?"

"I don't know, Ed. I swear I don't at this moment know."

"All right, maybe you're telling the truth."

"I couldn't lie to you, Ed." Her smile became a giggle. "You might find out and beat me."

"Giles might do worse than that if he learns you're selling him out."

"How can he ever know? You won't tell him."

"No."

"Then he can't find out." She picked up a handbag that had a shoulder strap. She put the strap over her shoulder.

"My address is 4318 Royal Palm Boulevard, Ed—in case you want to talk to me about Giles."

"I'll remember," I said. "Wally Tulman ever get to that address?"

"Maybe."

"Often?"

"No—only once."

"Laura Tulman find out?"

"There was nothing to find out. One night—not long before that little girl was killed—Wally was in the Yacht Club bar drinking alone. It was a dull evening. I had nothing better to do."

"So you picked him up."

"Well," she said, "let's say I let him pick me up."

"Yeah?"

"We had a few drinks. He wasn't feeling so good. His

.self-confidence was about gone. Worried and suffering because he felt he'd made a mess of things. Now Giles could have taken Wally's plush-lined slot and had the time of his life with everything he wanted. Isn't that life for you? Giles really would make some rich female a devoted, gay, companionable lap dog—he'd honestly try to make her happy. And there was Wally, in the very spot Giles wanted, making himself and his wife miserable because he couldn't relax and take things as they were. He had to be punishing himself because he had got to think of himself as a failure, as not much of a man."

Evie sighed. "Well, Wally needed somebody to talk to. So he talked. And he drank. And finally the liquor in him began seeing me as a woman.

"We went for a drive. And when he took me to the cottage, he just got out of the car and came on in. I figured it for a usual evening. He was well heeled and old enough to know what he wanted."

"But it wasn't a usual evening?"

"Nope," Evie Grove said with her light laugh. "She fooled me."

"Who did?"

"Laura Tulman, you dummy. I told Wally to mix us a drink while I got into something more comfortable. When I came back to the living area, he was gone. First and only time I ever had one of them take off from the cottage to go home."

"Maybe his flesh was willing but his conscience wasn't."

She tipped her head to one side. "You wouldn't think much of it one way or the other."

"Maybe. Maybe not."

She dropped the shoulder-strap handbag and sat on the day bed. "What's to think about? The appetites of the body are real and normal."

"Civilized, too," I said, "if disciplined."

With a gay toss of her hair, she burst into laughter. "A Puritan, no less."

"No. You couldn't understand what Wally Tulman did. I was explaining it for you."

"Oh, who can explain a monstrous little snake who'd fear a woman and molest a child?"

"I don't think he feared you. I think he had a lot more courage than even he thinks. The more I see of this thing, the more I think they've got the wrong man in Raiford. I'm the man who'd fear you, not Wally."

"You?" she said, her eyes wide. She touched her lips with her tongue, a hint of pleasure in her face.

"Sure," I said. "You got a chunk missing inside of you."

"Have I? Really?"

"You've lost the line between right and wrong, Evie."

"Dear, dear," she said.

I shrugged. "It's none of my business."

"No, tell me. This I must hear. I didn't know there were any men left around like you. The ones I meet are afraid of something or running from something or trying to prove something. You don't need to prove anything and you wouldn't run from a bulldozer if you got good and sore at it."

"I've run from mere men," I said. "Don't kid yourself on that score. I'd run from some women just as quick, maybe a lot quicker."

"Quit running from me, Ed."

"Why?"

"Suddenly I like you. You're different. I find you exciting." She glanced around the room. She sniffed, crinkled her nose. "Faint sweat. Faint smell of old beer cans. Faint smell of an animal's lair."

"Yeah," I said, "and the wary animal is wondering who pointed out the cave."

"I've explained my motives, Ed."

"You've given some excuses. Who are you really?"

"Just a woman who was brought up in luxury. Then my father lost all his money. He and my mother died. I was left penniless. But not helpless. I like money, Ed. There's a way of living that I like. Does that answer your question?"

"Who told you I was on this case?"

A slow smile came to her face. "So that's what's worrying you. Well, the answer is simple. Juan told me."

"Who is Juan?"

"The bartender at the Yacht Club bar. He served you a beer and Milt Collins was there and he witnessed your run-in with Milt."

She stood up. I put my arm around her waist. Her flesh was firm and yielding. She had what it took to interest the millionaires.

"Ed . . ."

"Shut up," I said.

"Yes, Ed."

CHAPTER

7

SHE KNEW how to kiss a man. She drew her face back, hit me lightly on the mouth with her lips again, and said, "Why didn't I meet up with you a long time ago? Now how about a drink?"

"All I got's beer."

"Oh."

"There's a package store on the corner," I said.

"Fine. We'll have a party."

I went out of the building and bought a bottle of Scotch at the corner store.

As I came back, I spotted the man on the other side of the street. He was in shadows. You wouldn't have seen him. I did. My habits are different.

I figured he might have a buddy on down the street or maybe on my side of the street, but I didn't spot a second one.

Without breaking pace or letting him know I'd seen him, I turned into the house and moved up the stairs to the apartment.

When I went in, Evie Grove was lounging on the day bed. She'd combed out that honey mist of hair and put fresh lipstick on.

She'd got out ice and a bottle of ginger ale that had been kicking around in the refrigerator.

"Scotch?" she said. "I'll have mine on the rocks, Ed."

"Later."

"What?"

"The party's postponed."

She swung her feet to the floor and jerked herself upright.

"Before you blow your stack," I said, "let me ask you if you were ever in jail?"

"No."

"It isn't pleasant."

"What's jail got to do with us?"

"Maybe nothing. Maybe I've turned into a cautious old man. But if you want to save yourself—and me—some trouble, you'd better get out."

"Ed—"

"It isn't a brush-off. You'll leave with my regrets. That help?"

"A little."

"Just ease out the back way. Cross through the alley to the next street. Catch a cab. Go home."

She took a moment to study my face. Then her smile flashed. "Good night, Ed."

I took her arm and guided her to the door. I opened the door and steered her toward the back stairway. I watched her slick figure disappear into the gloom of the rear stairs. Then I closed the door, put the Scotch on a shelf in the kitchenette, opened a beer, turned off the light and sat down to wait.

A considerable time passed. I'd about decided I was wrong. He could have been watching the house because of somebody else.

Then I heard the faint whisper of the floor in the hallway.

Looking at the spot in the darkness where the door was supposed to be, I gave a short, soft laugh. Like a laugh of pleasure. Like I was laughing with someone.

A couple hundred pounds of beef hit the door. The hinges held, but the latch didn't.

I clicked on the light, leveled the .38 at him.

"You make one move," I said, "and I'll pin a brand new belly button on you."

It was Garcia, a workhorse flatfoot. His swarthy face went as pale as possible, and his coal-black eyes jolted halfway out of their sockets. The leer on his face went plain sick.

He took his hand gingerly out of his coat pockets, leaving flashlight and gun in the pockets.

"You got a warrant?" I asked.

He stared.

I said, "I could shoot you with impunity, tearing in here like this."

He shook his head. He didn't believe I'd be drastic, but he wasn't absolutely sure.

"Anybody can make a mistake, Ed," he managed at last.

"Not like this," I said. "Turn around."

"Where we going?"

"To headquarters. That's where you intended me to go, isn't it? The woman and me."

He turned and we went out of the apartment. In the sultry darkness over the street, I said, "Where's your car?"

"Right over there."

"You're the chauffeur," I said. "After all, it's only taxpayer's money buying your time, the car, the gasoline, the organization."

We walked across the street and got in the black police car.

"Ignore the two-way," I said.

Garcia kept casting sidelong glances at me as we drove to the municipal building. By the time we parked the car, his mind was off me. He was sweating like a ward heeler losing an election. I knew he was thinking ahead—to his carpeting with Julian Patrick.

The desk sergeant got to his feet when Garcia and I walked in.

I told Garcia, "You've got as cute as you're ever going to get with me. Don't try it again."

The desk sergeant was looking from one to the other of us.

"Tell Julian Patrick that Ed Rivers has brought Garcia in. Then place this man under arrest for trespassing, forcible entry and violation of privacy."

"Now look, Ed—" Garcia said.

"Shut up."

"Are you kidding?" the desk sergeant said. He was a young, strapping, sandy guy. Not on the force long enough to lose his sense of humor. He was having trouble keeping his smile under control.

"No," I said, "I'm not kidding. I arrested this man under the powers granted to me by the State of Florida in issuance of a private detective's license, and also under the powers granted by the Constitution of the United States, which authorizes a private citizen to make an arrest if present upon and during the commission of a crime. I'll sign the complaint and appear as State's witness."

"By God," Garcia blustered. "Who the hell you think—"

"I told you to shut up. Now, Sergeant, you better get Patrick out here."

"I can't do that, Mr. Rivers."

"Why not?"

"Lieutenant Patrick is attending a party at the home of the mayor."

"Don't explain the trouble to His Honor," I said. "Or he might want to tag along and he'd just be in the way. Tell Patrick to think about his position in the city of Tampa. I'll wait in his office and give him thirty minutes to get here."

No matter what he was feeling inside, Patrick never changed on the outside. He was as cool as a knife blade, unhurried and calm when he walked into his office.

A tall, slender man, he moved with the grace of a dancer. His face was a little too narrow to be handsome, but a lot of women didn't seem to mind. He had polished black hair and polished black eyes and a polished black mustache that went with the polish of his white and black evening clothes.

"Hello, Ed," he said, going around behind his desk. He sat down and rocked back, showing no irritation, no worry, no apparent interest.

"Your man's been locked up," I said.

"He'll be fined. Not because of you, Ed, but because he was incompetent."

"That's too bad. You knew Laura Tulman was going to hire a private eye. You knew the moment she hired me. Maybe you jumped the gun a little."

"I don't believe I understand that last remark, Ed."

"Maybe it was Garcia who slugged me in the vestibule of my apartment building and followed it up with a phone call trying to scare me off."

"Sorry," he said. "You're wrong on that."

"Okay. But he's been on my tail from just about that moment. Tonight he saw a known prostitute go to my apartment. He stationed himself outside. He saw me arrive. He saw that she apparently stayed. I guess he got a lot of big dreams about promotion—or maybe he phoned you and it was you who dreamed up the gimmick."

"I don't follow you, Ed."

"The hell you don't! If Garcia had found what he was so certain he would find in that apartment, he'd have hauled me and a naked chippy down here, slapped a morals charge against us, and handed you my license on a silver platter. You'd have put me out of business, all right, Julie, and out of the Tulman case for keeps."

"You might have got your license back."

"By being reasonable?"

Patrick shrugged.

I splayed my fingers on his desk and leaned toward him.

"That's a dirty way of fighting, Julie." I could feel myself losing my temper. Nobody ever lost his temper with Patrick and won.

"Are we fighting, Ed? I didn't know we were fighting."

I straightened and took a breath. "Okay, so I don't let you sucker me into saying or doing something that still might land me upstairs in the cooler and put an arrest on my record."

"You want an apology from Garcia?"

"I don't give a damn about Garcia," I said. "Kick him off the force and he'll go back where he belongs, to peddling *bolita* or picking Spanish fly. It'd be good for the city to have him in a spot where he can do only minor damage."

Patrick smiled. He had a way of smiling. It changed his whole face and personality. It lighted him up like the flow of light from gentle candles had suddenly surrounded him. It made him your friend.

"I don't blame you for being sore, Ed. Maybe we can make it up to you."

"You could, but you won't."

"How could I? Try me. I might surprise you."

"What's with this Tulman case, Julie?"

"Nothing."

"See, I said—"

He held up his hand to stop me. "Take it easy, Ed. I'm telling you the truth. We had the guy dead to rights. He's where he belongs."

"But you don't want me on the case."

"No," he said, "I don't. But that doesn't mean there's the slightest doubt of Wallace Tulman's guilt. It simply means that I know you for what you are. You're bullheaded, and you'll raise questions. As questions could be raised about any case. You'll throw the whole mess into the papers, and we don't want that. In any other case, it wouldn't matter. But the nature of this case, and the people involved, are different. I'd take almost any measures to keep you from lighting a fire under this pot again, Ed."

"Okay, Julie. I'm beginning to see the light. I've watched you for a long time. I've seen a once-nice guy become cynical. I've witnessed the decay spread out inside of you. You're rising, Julie. You're getting to be a big man. One by one you're putting the politicians and rats in your back pocket.

"Ambition's a sickness with you, Julie. You intend to be the master and dictator of this city, and the goal seems in reach now, doesn't it? With old lady Wherry's power, prestige and money behind you, you feel like you got it made. The way you handled the Tulman case made you that old gal's fair-haired boy—and her shadow falls long over City Hall.

"But I'll tell you something, Julie. I'm very sorry for you."

I turned and walked out of the office. As I was closing the door, Julian Patrick said softly, "Ed . . ."

It was my last chance to turn back. I couldn't, even if I had wanted to. I'd asked for no part in this thing; it had fallen on me like a ton of bricks in the dark vestibule of my apartment house.

I closed Patrick's office door behind me.

I turned left and went to the press room. Two reporters were there, shooting the breeze and drinking coffee out of paper cartons.

I knew them both.

"Hello, boys," I said. "I got a little item for you."

CHAPTER

8

SITTING opposite me in a quiet restaurant, Laura Tulman was more than beautiful. Today she wore yellow and the color darkened her already black hair and eyes. It did things for the smooth tan of her face and the full deep redness of her lips. For my money, if you traced her line back, you'd find some of the best blood in southern Europe. Castile maybe.

She folded the newspaper, laid it down as if it was red hot, and smiled at me across her lunch coffee.

"Do you always go off with such a resounding explosion, Ed?"

I glanced at the paper. It was all there, front-page stuff with plenty of pictures dug up out of newspaper files.

I shrugged. "I didn't do a thing, except tell the reporters I was on the case and answer their questions."

"And such thorough questions. They got it all, from the assault on you at your apartment house to the effort by Lieutenant Patrick to discredit you and get you off the case.

With the nature of the charge against Wally, it all adds up to a few questions and some very sensational stuff."

"I guess it does. I hope I don't meet the fate Julie Patrick must be wishing on me right now."

"But he's not a part of your purpose, and you always have a purpose, don't you?"

"I try to."

"The purpose is Giles Newell," she said.

"You got brains as well as beauty."

"The papers are calling him the vanishing witness. It doesn't look good, from his point of view."

"That's too bad," I said.

"It might frighten him."

"I'm pretty sure it will."

"He might run to a point beyond discovery."

"Not if he's as canny as he's been pictured to me. When a building burns, all kind of creatures come scurrying out. Some that you didn't even know were there. But we're not going to wait for Giles to get a hotfoot. We're going to keep looking. That's why I asked you to lunch. You know him, his habits."

"Not very well."

"Better than I do. I want you to help."

"All I can," she said. She sat with her elbows on the table, her chin resting on her clasped hands. "Was she really beautiful, Ed?"

"Evie Grove?"

"Who else?"

"She sure as hell was."

Her eyes deepened and changed expression. But I couldn't read her.

Skip to dinner. The afternoon would have bored you stiff, unless you like legwork through snarling traffic and heat that clogged the throat and writhed in the guts.

Laura Tulman was game. She stuck with me. At dinner

she still looked neat and reasonably fresh, though I knew she was dish-rag limp and her feet were pumping with a tortured life of their own.

We ate in the heart of town, at a Franklin Street restaurant. The noise of the city was subdued and far away. The air-conditioning began putting new life in battered cells. The drinks were tall and cool and the food good.

I laid the scanty notes I'd taken on the table between us. She looked at the dog-eared bit of paper and said, "Not a lot to show for the afternoon."

"I've had worse days."

"So have I, Ed." She looked at me quietly as she said it. I didn't know exactly how she meant it. She wasn't an indirect person. I decided she meant it the way I'd like for her to mean it.

I looked at her, and there was no sentiment between us. The thing that came to life and writhed invisibly in and around us was as vivid as a woman damp and dark with loveliness in a hot Florida night.

She cut her eyes away. "We didn't find out much about Giles, did we?"

"I guess we didn't," I said.

We were off the hook now and the feeling passed. She picked up the notes and studied them. She needed to do something with her hands.

She read them over, as if expecting to find something hidden, something I hadn't written at all. She didn't find anything, of course. Only that Giles Newell had left his apartment and given no forwarding address. Only that no telephone or gas or electric service had been extended to him in Tampa since he'd left his last known address. Only that he hadn't contacted any of his few known friends.

We'd found one thing.

He had a sister.

We got that from a bartender at the big Spanish restaurant in Ybor City. This restaurant is quite a famous tourist attraction and the waiters and musicians are high-toned folks. Their union included employees at such spots as the Yacht Club bar, and this barkeep and Giles had once worked a Sarasota place together.

Giles's sister had been a real dish in those days. Her name was Carrie. Carrie Hofstetter. She'd married a mug in Miami she thought was a businessman. He turned out to be a racetrack tout. They followed the nags north and south for a few seasons and he got in trouble with a gambling syndicate.

Hofstetter went one way and Carrie the other. She'd showed up in Sarasota while Giles was working there. She looked like a lady, but she was long-gone lush. With a few drinks under her girdle she turned into a first-class bat. Giles had cut off the help he was giving her, and she had come to the bar and made two or three scenes that were lulus. Giles had lost his job because of it. He'd drifted to Tampa and nobody heard of Carrie for a while. Then she'd turned up in Tampa also, and was living in a place in West Tampa.

The bartender hadn't known her address. I'd got it at headquarters. She was a regular inmate of the city jail on public drunk charges. She'd been booked once on suspicion of auto theft. Twice for assault and battery. Once on suspicion of dope peddling. She'd been fined, pulled a couple of short-term sentences and remained a little part in that morass of human flotsam the police wearily accept as chronic headaches.

I didn't run into Julie Patrick at headquarters. Nobody said anything about him to me. On the surface, my relation with the official body was the same. Garcia, I learned, had been temporarily relieved of duty.

I figured Garcia would be back to shaking down dirty-picture peddlers in about sixty days. There wasn't much I could do about that. I was no Sir Galahad jousting for the city of Tampa. The city of Tampa could damn well take care of itself—as long as it didn't step on my toes when I was working in the interests of a client. In that case, I'd do what I could to move forward unimpeded. And I figured Julie Patrick would think twice now before trying to gum me further on the Tulman case. He was too big a man, too juicy a target for the papers to rip to pieces.

I drank a beer while Laura Tulman finished an after-dinner brandy. I paid the check, and we went out into the bustle and swelter of Franklin Street. I whistled down a taxi and gave him the West Tampa address.

We crossed the Hillsborough River, which, with the rail-road tracks, slice up downtown Tampa and make it a hell of a place to get around in. For a moment the air was clean. Then we went quickly into West Tampa.

We passed shacks that should have been condemned, and joints where trouble often is no farther away than the swish of a switch-blade knife.

The address was a five-story firetrap on a corner.

"Wait," I told the cabbie, and he slouched behind the wheel and dropped his cap over his dark Cuban eyes.

Laura and I crossed the sidewalk. A couple of guys lounging in the doorway of the building found her pretty easy to look at. I shouldered them aside, and we stepped into the foyer.

The paint was peeling on the walls, and the plaster was cracked. The row of mailboxes was battered, and some of them lacked names.

Her name had been scrawled in ink on a bit of card-board and slotted on one of the boxes.

Carrie Hofstetter. 514.

We walked up the five flights. There were plenty of kids in the building. You could hear their chatter and cries. A guy was cursing them on the second, and the heat brought the stench of their urine out of a partially opened door on the third.

I wondered if she ever remembered the days at Hialeah.

Five fourteen was a front corner apartment. I knocked, and the door was opened immediately.

She was a bloated redhead, gone the way only a good-looking, delicate redhead can go. Her puffy, soft body was clad in a greasy wrapper. Her hair was a stringy mop. The prettiness of her face had all dripped and run out of shape. Yet there was still a hint of it there. If your imagination could pull the sags and straighten the lines, you could see that she'd once been very pretty. The kind of delicate prettiness that you find in a face with blue shadows under the eyes. The kind that's easily destroyed.

"Mrs. Hofstetter?"

She nodded. She was holding the wrapper with her hands. It clung enough to show that she still had a figure of sorts. Like her face, it had run at the edges.

"My name is Rivers," I said. "I'd appreciate it if I could talk to you for a minute."

"Well, I'm busy. I was getting dressed to go out."

She'd opened the door like she was expecting somebody.

"This won't take long," I said, "and it's very important."

"Well, all right." She glanced at Laura. Furtively, she caught the length of Laura and there was the briefest pang of regret and hate in her eyes.

"This is Mrs. Tulman," I said. "If you don't mind, we'd like to talk inside."

"I really haven't long."

She let us in and closed the door. The apartment was close, hot, dense with the smell of powder, whisky, and heavy perfume. We were in a living room furnished with an old wicker set. Through an open door I could glimpse a bedroom with all the blinds closed and an unmade bed.

Carrie Hofstetter sat on the edge of a wicker chair. She was nervous. Her glance drifted toward a rickety wicker table holding a fifth of whisky and some scaly-looking glasses.

"Would you care for a drink?" she asked hopefully.

Laura and I shook our heads. I said, "We just had dinner, but why don't you go ahead?"

"If you don't mind," she mumbled. She got up, went to the table, and poured herself a stiff drink. Her hand was shaking a little.

She threw that one down the hatch without batting a lash. She poured a second, bigger than the first, and brought it back to her chair.

"What·was it you wanted, Mr. Rivers?"

"I want to see Giles," I said.

Her eyes went bright, then cloudy. "What makes you think he's here?"

"I don't. But he's your brother. You know where he is, don't you?"

"No. I'm sorry, I don't."

She was lying.

"It's very important that I see him, Mrs. Hofstetter."

"He don't have anything much to do with me."

"I see. Have you seen the papers today?"

"No, I only just got up."

"Giles figures in them."

She paled a little. But she tried not to show any feeling. "What's he done?"

"Nothing. That's the whole trouble. You know he testified at the Tulman trial."

"Sure, I know all that. What's he done now? What's with this stuff in the papers today?"

"It still concerns the Tulman case, Mrs. Hofstetter."

I could see fright taking form in her eyes. "Yeah? Who are you anyway, a cop?"

"A private cop."

She glanced from me to Laura and back again. "I get it. But you lay off Giles, you hear!"

"You think a great deal of your brother."

"Never mind that. Just leave him alone, I say!"

I watched her expression. A few things added up. She

knew more than she was telling. Giles was her last prop, her final means of support. She saw trouble forming up for him, trouble that might leave her facing the world alone, and it scared the panties off her.

"You get out of here!" she yelled. "The both of you!"

"Okay," I said. "If you value Giles's neck, you'll have a little talk with him. About a big question mark that's been dropped in the Tulman case. About his testimony."

"I already told you—"

"Sure," I said. "Just mention it to him when you see him at this spot where you don't know where he is."

Laura and I went out. I knew she was glad to escape the building. I helped her into the waiting taxi and told the driver to pull around the corner.

When the cab stopped after the half-block haul, I told Laura, "You might as well go on home."

"No, Ed, I'll wait. I'd rather."

"All right," I said.

I looked around and spotted a convenient doorway. I took my heat-blistered feet over there.

All I did was run up a big taxi bill. Carrie Hofstetter was no dummy. She couldn't see me, but she knew I was out there. She stuck inside her building with the tenacity of the cockroaches.

CHAPTER

9

It was almost midnight when I took Laura home. She was tired and quiet as she keyed open the front door.

"Keep your chin up," I said. "It's been a long, rough

day, but you never know about such days. We might have accomplished a lot more than it seems right now."

"I expected this to take time, Ed," she said. "Would you like a drink before you go home?"

"Have you got some beer?"

"I think so."

I stepped to the driveway and told the cabbie he could go.

Laura had gone inside the house and turned on the lights in the living area. It was tricky lighting, soft, diffused. The sprawling, spacious luxury of the home could have had no other lighting.

"I'll only be a minute, Ed."

While she went to powder her nose, I sank down in one of the big, square chairs. It didn't look comfortable, but it was.

I didn't have much chance to get settled in it. A scream came from the wing of the house where Laura had gone.

I got out of the chair fast. An opening in the end of the living area gave access to a hallway. Down the hallway, a door was standing open, throwing an oblong of light in the hall.

Beyond the lighted door, there was a crash. Another scream, quickly muffled this time. And a burst of wild laughter.

I reached the bedroom door and shot inside the room. A slender young woman was trying to carve Laura up with a butcher knife. Laura had her fingers locked about the woman's wrist. She was bigger and stronger than the other woman, but she couldn't break the grip on the knife.

As I stepped up to them, the woman tore loose from Laura and made a lunge at me. Her thin, sensitive face, misted in a cloud of blond hair, was as blood-hungry as a starving Everglades panther's.

She didn't know how to fight with a knife. She came in

slashing from every direction at once. She had only this crazy strength and the desire to kill.

I grabbed at the arm swinging the knife. She was too quick for me. The tip of the knife laid a furrow down my forearm. As the blood spurted down my arm, she cackled in her throat and shot the knife toward my face. I threw my arm up, crossed with my other hand, and grabbed her wrist.

She flopped and floundered in my grasp like a fear-maddened fish on a line. Suddenly, she was screaming shrilly.

"Let me go, please let me go!"

I snapped her arm around hard and she dropped the knife. When it left her grasp, her mood changed again. She used her free hand to claw at my eyes. She began mouthing some very unladylike words. They didn't make sense. They were disjointed brickbats of filth.

I threw my free arm about her tiny waist and turned her back to me. She kicked my shins. Then her head came jerking around and she tried to grind her teeth together in the flesh of my cheek.

I ducked my head, hung onto her writhing, sweatslick form, and said, "Spread a sheet on the bed, Laura!"

The struggling girl hammered an elbow against my ribs as Laura riffled a sheet over the bed.

I threw the girl down hard on the sheet. She grabbed the edge of the bed and tried to crawl away. I jerked her hands back, wedged them against her sides, and threw her body over. She began kicking, methodically and hard.

I got the end of the sheet over her and started rolling her in it.

"No, no, no!" she screamed, each word higher.

She arched her back until it seemed her spine would break. She went limp suddenly, throwing me off balance. Her face twisted about, her fine, even teeth snapping. She was anything but beautiful now. Still wistful, still hauntingly delicate. But her hair was plastered about her face, her eyes were bottomless. She was something right out of a Freudian nightmare.

Over the years, I've had to take on what was thrown at me. I never wanted to, never asked for it. Some of the trouble that's come my way has been big and tough. I've always managed.

But this little woman was a new chapter in the book. She got those teeth in the lobe of my ear and nearly tore the ear off. She put a knee in my crotch and I went blind for a second with the pain.

She was whipping the hell out of me.

I was too busy trying to keep the storm from bursting all over me to take my hands off her. So I jerked my ear lobe free and butted her.

I hit her hard with the top of my head right under the point of her chin.

She gagged briefly. Then she was limp.

I reeled from the bed. My arm was burning where the knife had laid the furrow. My crotch was pumping, like it was swelling to twice its normal size. My ear was numb. I touched it to make sure it was still there.

I stood gasping for breath with sweat rivering down my face.

"It's Stephanie Collins, Ed," Laura said. Her voice was quiet and sad.

I looked at Mrs. Collins in repose. A little of that elusive beauty had come back to the hollow cheeks and the hollows about the closed eyes. Looking at her, you knew she'd always been finely tuned. And it was easy to realize what the death, and the manner of the death, of her little girl had done to her.

Laura touched my arm and looked at my ear. "You need some doctoring fast, Ed."

"It'll hold for a second," I said.

I rolled Stephanie Collins in the sheet. Then I told

Laura to get a couple more sheets from the linen closet. I ripped those into six long bands and bound Stephanie Collins snugly in the makeshift strait jacket.

The bleeding had just about stopped on my arm and ear. My crotch pain had eased so that I figured I still had my manhood.

I followed Laura into the bathroom and she washed the blood off my arm and ear. Then she swabbed the wounds with merthiolate. She wrapped the arm in gauze and taped it down. The ear, I decided, didn't need a bandage.

Stephanie Collins had come out of it when we went back in the bedroom. Every muscle was rigid against the homemade strait jacket. She looked at me and I had the feeling the lids of her eyes were going to strain wrong side out.

"Rape you," she said.

"Mrs. Collins . . ."

"Ruthie was raped," she said.

"Stephanie . . ." Laura said with a break in her voice.

Stephanie Collins turned her burning eyes in the direction of Laura's voice. "Rape," she said.

"Don't you know me, Stephanie?" Laura cried.

"Rape," Stephanie Collins said.

She lapsed into thought for a second. Then she whispered the word and began laughing. The laughter broke off as quickly as it had started. A blob of spit came rolling out the side of her mouth.

"He raped Ruthie," she said. "The dirty little rat."

She repeated the phrases in a singsong voice, gradually built them into a weird melody.

Laura was standing with the knuckles of her hand pressed against her mouth.

"Laura," I said.

Slowly she looked at me.

"Do you know the hospital?" I asked.

Her gaze was impelled again to Stephanie Collins. She shook her head. Her face was gray and ill with grief. "The family slipped her away quietly when she tried to kill herself after Ruthie's death."

"Kill myself," Stephanie Collins said. "Kill Ruthie . . . I'll kill you . . . Where is the pretty knife?" She rolled her head from side to side.

"Better get Milt Collins over here," I told Laura, "if he's home."

Laura nodded and went out. I moved to the open window and wished we could get some breeze tonight.

The room became very quiet.

Stephanie Collins giggled. I looked at her over my shoulder. Her eyes were furtive and cunning.

"Is Mother here yet?"

"Not yet, Mrs. Collins."

"I do wish she'd hurry. We'll be late for the party. You're coming to the party with us, aren't you?"

"Yes, Mrs. Collins."

"Do you know," she whispered, "that while we're at the party Ruthie will be raped and murdered?"

I didn't know how to play along with this. I didn't want to get her upset again. I wished Laura would get back with Milt Collins.

"Do I know you?" she rambled, frowning suddenly.

"I'm Ed Rivers," I said.

"Are you a friend of Max the Giant's?"

"Well, I've met him."

"Are you a freak like the others?"

"No, Mrs. Collins."

"Did you know Father's a freak?"

"I didn't know him," I said.

"Oh, not outside." She thought a moment and giggled. "It doesn't show with Father. He's a freak inside. Like me . . . like me . . ."

The flame abated in her eyes. For a moment her eyes were almost sane. She moved against the strait jacket. But she didn't struggle. She simply seemed to realize that it was there and something was horribly wrong. Her moan was worse than any scream could have been.

She closed her eyes and began sobbing brokenly. The wet hair lay delicately, wispy gold, against the soft skin of her forehead.

I heard footsteps in the hallway. Laura and Milt Collins came into the room.

The big, outdoorsy, handsome man looked at his wife and years of time crept over his face.

"I'll help you get her home," I volunteered.

He nodded and gestured vaguely with his hand as if too tired to speak.

I picked up Stephanie Collins. I was ready for an outburst, but she lay draped across my arms as light and supine as a child.

Milt Collins started out of the room. As I followed him, I looked at Laura. "I'll still have that beer."

She brought a weak smile to her lips and nodded.

I trailed Milt Collins across the wide lawns separating the two houses. He held the door for me and I carried Stephanie Collins inside her own home.

Young Bryan was standing sturdily in the middle of the living area. He looked calmly at his mother's face.

"Go watch the television in the den," his father told him shortly.

"Yes, Father." He turned and marched out of the room.

"We'll put her in bed," Milt Collins said, "and I'll call the hospital."

The phone rang.

"Just a minute," Collins said.

He picked up the ivory living-room extension phone. From his end of the conversation, I knew it was the hospital calling him.

He shook off some of the lethargy that gripped him. He was a driving, hard-boiled man for a few minutes. He gave them hell. He called them incompetents and gave orders for someone to stay with her night and day. Yes, his wife was here, safe, no thanks to them. If they permitted her to escape again, he'd not only sue the pants off them, he'd take the place apart a plank at a time, personally.

He cradled the phone, pulled a handkerchief from his hip pocket, and wiped his face.

"They're on their way, Rivers," he said. "Just put her on the couch."

I put her on the couch. He moved as if he would touch her. But he didn't. He looked at her a minute, raw hell in his eyes.

Then with an effort of will, he turned his face from her.

"Thanks, Rivers," he said.

"You're welcome," I said.

He looked me over. Sober now, he looked me over as if he were seeing me for the first time.

"I suppose I made a fool of myself at the Yacht Club bar," he said.

"Yes, you did."

"I apologize," he said simply.

I liked the apology. It was laid on the line without insolence or undue humility.

I nodded. Then I briefed him on what had happened in the Tulman house. He listened without changing expression.

"I suppose," he said, "it's a good thing you stayed on the case this long. Stephanie might have killed Laura Tulman."

He walked over to a blond portable bar and poured himself a drink. "I owe you something, Rivers."

"My charges are seventy-five dollars a day and expenses."

"I'll send you a check for a day's pay tomorrow morning."

"All right," I said, "in this instance I believe I've earned it. Here's my card."

He took the card, looked at it, downed his drink and returned to the bar to pour himself a second. "I could make the check much bigger, Rivers."

"No, thanks."

"Why not?"

"I'm not dropping the Tulman case," I said. "I'm getting tired of explaining that to people."

His face pinked. "I'm accustomed to getting my way, Rivers."

"You ought to get over that. It can lead to frustration."

His color got a shade hotter than pink. "And what do you think you'll get out of all this?"

"I don't know. A fee."

"If it's a fee you're interested in—"

"A fee is what I work for. It isn't the whole end that I live for."

"Oh," he sneered. "An idealist."

I laughed aloud. "I've been called everything else, Collins. Never that."

"Damned if I understand you."

"Skip it. Maybe you never will. People pile up fees because they're afraid of tomorrow. But I'm not afraid of tomorrow, Collins, and I've got a job to do today."

"You're asking for plenty of trouble. You're not dealing with an Ybor City punk!"

"Well, that's all right," I said. "I hope your wife gets along better after this."

I started out of the room.

"Rivers!"

I stopped and turned.

Collins was standing spread-legged in the middle of the room. A struggle showed in his face. Then the lines of his face went loose and he looked tired and old.

"I've never said please in my adult life, Rivers. I'm saying it now. Please. Let it lie. Let my family alone."

"I don't want to hurt your family," I said. "You must know that."

"You've hurt them already. All that rehash of the case in the papers this morning. And for what? So you can earn a fee? That's all you'll ever find. They've got the right man in Raiford. They've found out everything that can be found out. So, please. I can't have my family . . ."

He broke off. Looking at my face, he twisted his lips in a spasm of helplessness. "Damn you to hell," he said softly.

He threw the highball glass with all his strength. I ducked it. It smashed against the wall and its broken bits tinkled to the floor.

The sound roused Stephanie Collins. She began straining against the makeshift strait jacket.

Milt Collins dropped on the couch beside her. She was whispering meaningless words, her eyes wide and staring at images of their own. He pressed her face against his chest and held her body tightly against him. After a few seconds I realized he was crying.

When I went outside, a black Caddy limousine drew to a stop in the driveway. Max the Giant got out and opened the rear door for Mrs. Wherry. The old lady stepped from the car briskly.

She gave me a dour look as she brushed past me. She and the mountainous man with the pink seal's head went inside the house. I guessed the hospital had called her, along with their call to Collins.

CHAPTER

10

LAURA opened beer and set it before me. Then she sat beside me on the couch, her legs tucked under her. The soft lighting in the living room brought shadows to her face. Or maybe the day had put them there.

"She was resting quietly and the hospital had somebody on the way," I said.

Laura looked through the floor-to-ceiling windows in the general direction of the Collins house. Then she got up and drew the drapes closed over the windows.

She stood before me, the light at her back. A sudden choked sound came from her throat. "I need somebody, Ed! My God, how I need somebody!"

She stood, and a shudder ran over her body.

"I'm so tired," she said. "For years I've had to have strength. I had to be a businesswoman. I had to be a snug haven for a gentle man-child. I had to be his source of strength. I had to do the spiritual fighting for him all during the trial. I was brought up on hard discipline, a sense of duty, Ed Rivers. Maybe that part of me attached me to Wally. But now I'm tired. The strength is gone and the spirit's drooping."

She put her hands over her face. But she didn't make a sound. She stood swaying.

I set the beer down and stood up. I took her wrists in my hands and pulled her hands away from her face.

"Stephanie Collins upset you."

"Yes, she did. But it's more than that."

The sweat heat of my body rose between us. We stood without saying anything. Then I put my fingers in the shiny black wealth of her hair and kissed her.

She didn't struggle. She flowed against me and her arms went around my neck. Her lips had a heat of their own, and I could sense and feel something stirring deep inside of her. Somehow I knew it was something that had never been touched before, never stirred before.

It was exactly as I had known it would be. Maybe in the back of my mind I'd known it from the first. I hadn't consciously thought of it before. But now I did. My blood was thick and heavy. And I knew this conscious thought was only the visible part of a thought that had been in my mind from the minute I'd laid eyes on her.

I could feel her fingernails savage on my shoulders. Not the touch Wally had known.

"You're elemental, Ed."

"I guess."

"An animal. A bear. A cross between a swamp panther and a bear."

"I don't need protecting—by a woman."

"You sure as hell don't," she said.

Then she broke away from me. She stood with her face flushed and the hair tumbled about her cheeks.

I took a step toward her.

"No, Ed!"

"Yes," I said.

"No," she said, almost wildly. "Leave, Ed. Now."

"Laura—"

"Don't talk," she said. "Just leave. That wasn't a cheap play I made just now. I didn't mean it as a cheap play."

"I know it wasn't. And I'm not playing cheap, Laura."

She was gasping. "Then leave. If you mean that, get out. For the sake of mercy, Ed, get out before I start begging you to stay!"

I walked to the door, opened it, walked through the doorway and closed the door behind me.

Then I walked hard and fast. I began to sweat hard, but I didn't care about the heat. I walked halfway to downtown Tampa. Then a taxi passed and I whistled him.

I rode over to the corner below my apartment building. I walked into the all-night market, and I must have looked okay.

The lean, dark, young night man said, "Hi, Mr. Rivers."

"Hello," I said.

"Ice?"

"That's right."

I paid for the twenty-five pound block of ice and carried it up to my apartment.

I put the ice in a dishpan and the dishpan on a table near the day bed. Then I set an electric fan behind the ice and turned the fan on.

I stripped to my shorts and lay down on the day bed. I didn't want to think.

But the ice had gone to water before I went to sleep.

I slept late. The ringing of the phone woke me. I rolled to a sitting position, heavy with sleep and the heat. I clicked the fan switch and stopped the useless effort of stirring humid air.

I picked up the phone. "Rivers speaking."

"Laura here," she said.

"How are you this morning?"

"I'm fine, Ed," she said, keeping her voice impersonal. "I wanted to mention something to you last night, but with Stephanie Collins showing up, I forgot."

"Okay," I said, "shoot."

"I was going to ask what you intended to do about Carrie Hofstetter."

"Put a shadow on her from one of the other agencies. She's smart, but she knows where Giles is, and I believe she knows more than that. The expense of putting on a man she doesn't know, wouldn't recognize—"

"I wouldn't mind the expense. But it's too late."

"Too late?"

"Have you seen the morning papers?"

"No."

"Carrie Hofstetter had an accident late last night. She fell out of her apartment window. The—the alley below was asphalt, Ed."

"Then she didn't live long?"

"She was killed instantly," Laura said.

I heard the intake of her breath.

"Ed . . ."

"Yes?"

"This means a great deal, doesn't it?"

"Maybe. Or maybe it means she got drunk and fell out the window."

"What are you going to do about it?"

"I'm going to see Patrick. And the remains. And wonder if Giles Newell might have done that to his own sister."

"I'm sure he couldn't have, Ed. I didn't know him well, but I'm certain he couldn't have."

"Okay," I said. "Then this might still make him turn up."

"You mean . . ."

"He might show up to claim the body," I said. "She didn't have anybody else. And I guess he didn't either when you come right down to it."

CHAPTER

11

PATRICK was as polite as ice waiting in a highball glass.

"Hello, Ed. Sit down."

I sat down. His desk was between us. He pushed a file folder toward me.

I picked up the folder. In it was a report on the death of Carrie Hofstetter.

I glanced at Patrick. His smile made his dark, slender face handsome. But it was a saturnine face—if you knew him.

"You'd get to the information one way or another," he

said. "Why let you annoy me any more than I can help? Take all the time you need digesting it, Ed."

"Thanks, I will."

I read the report over. Carrie Hofstetter had been found dead in the alley beside her apartment house. The discovery had been made by a workman employed by a building contractor. The man had stepped from his ground-floor apartment into the alley to put out some garbage as he was leaving for work. He had seen the crumpled body. His call had reached headquarters at 8:05. A squad car and ambulance had arrived on the scene at 8:13. Carrie Hofstetter had been dead about two hours. She died with the rising sun.

And no one had seen or heard a thing.

Her apartment was the messy nest of an alcoholic. There were no signs of struggle in the apartment reported. A window overlooking the alley was open, and a shag throw rug was crumpled on the floor near it.

"You got the picture?" Patrick said.

"I got what it says here," I said.

He smiled, clasped his hands, laid them on the desk, and leaned toward me. "Is that an insinuation?"

"No. I think the department is too smart to doctor the report."

"Why, thanks," he said thinly.

"You know she was Giles Newell's sister?"

"I can't see that it makes any difference."

"You know I was over there last night to see her?"

"Business or pleasure?" he said with a sneer.

"There wasn't much pleasure in her," I said.

"So maybe it wasn't accidental after all." Patrick raised his brows. "Could have been suicide. She suddenly got sick of it all. Drunk, depressed, she took a dive."

"You got it all fixed, haven't you, Julie?"

"I don't know what you mean."

I could feel the heat beating in my throat. "The hell

you don't. By this time there must be a question in your mind. But you won't admit it. You're the great Julian Patrick. You're going to have an iron hand over all the hoods and politicians in this city. King of Tampa—and you don't give a damn how you get there."

"I might have known you'd get hotheaded, Ed. It's going to be your undoing one of these days."

"But not yet, Julie. Not for a long time. Not until I do what I've been paid to do."

"Bravo," Julie said.

"Okay," I said. "But remember one thing, Julie. You got born with a part of you cannibal. The death of Wally Tulman wouldn't mean a thing to you. You closed a sensational case quickly and successfully. It put old lady Wherry solidly behind you, and she's quite an ally in your dealings with City Hall. It's a real bargain for Wally Tulman's death, hey, Julie?"

"Especially since he's guilty," Patrick said placidly.

"I don't believe it, Julie. Not any more. He's no friend. If he died, it would be a stranger dying. But it's up to me to undo what's been done to him."

"Well, you just go right ahead and do that, Ed. Now I've got some work to do."

He pulled some papers on his desk toward him. I stood up. My hands were shaking. You couldn't reach Julie. And you can't fight a guy you can't reach.

I mopped some sweat off my face and headed for the door.

"Take care of yourself, Ed."

"I intend to."

"You're barking at shadows, of course. But if what you say is true, you'd better be careful. You could get killed, you know."

"Thanks for the warning."

"It isn't a warning. Just some simple, honest advice. Come back any time the department can co-operate with you, Ed."

"I'll do that, Julie."

"Fine." He raised his face and smiled at me. "I'll let the reporters know how we stand now. They'll want follow-ups for those stories they ran on your tip."

I resisted the impulse to slam the door behind me. But when I was outside headquarters, I still wanted to break something. There's nothing harder to beat your head against than shadows. I was ridden with the feeling that Julian Patrick was indestructible and whatever he wanted he would get.

I did a routine check at the morgue and took a taxi out to the Estates.

Laura answered my ring.

"Just in time for a late lunch," she said.

"I'm not hungry."

"Don't be a bear." She smiled.

Our eyes met, and the TNT that had almost gone off last night began quivering again.

"What did you find out?" she asked, turning away.

I followed her into the dining area where she set out sandwiches.

"They haven't had the inquest yet," I said, "but they'll rule it accidental death, sure as anything. The body is still in the morgue. Giles Newell hasn't claimed it yet."

"And what do you think, Ed? About her death, I mean."

"I don't know. The verdict of accidental death will hold up. Most factors point to it."

"Most factors?"

"There's one thing. I didn't mention it to Patrick. He's smart. Maybe he's already thought of it. If I knew for sure that he has, and if he doesn't bring it up at the inquest, then I'd know he's covering something. But I guess I'll never know for sure that he thought of this one angle."

"And what's the angle, Ed?"

"She didn't scream. Carrie Hofstetter fell from that top floor window without making an outcry. Falling people don't do that. Even a falling drunk lets out a bleat. If a drunk is too far gone to cry out, he couldn't very well walk by a window and fall out."

I picked up a ham on rye and took a bite. "If she jumped deliberately, she might not have yelled. So she either had to jump—or she was slugged and thrown from the window."

A shiver crossed Laura's shoulders. She started to push back her sandwich. Then resolutely she picked it up.

She was white about the lips. "Could our visit have triggered her death, Ed?"

"Yes."

"My God!"

"But don't feel bad about it. There had to be a condition for our visit to have done that. A condition of her own making. A condition that led to her death. So we're not responsible."

"I guess not."

"Let's think about Carrie Hofstetter for a minute," I said. "Since she split with her husband and faced the world alone, she's tagged and stuck with Giles like a rubber stamp on a mortgage foreclosure.

"He drifts from Sarasota to Tampa. She follows. He was her whole means of support, and apparently he suffered her, unable to bring himself to cut her off completely. This indicates that Giles in his own way needed her as much as she needed him. He needed somebody he could pour out his bellyaches to, somebody he could feel superior to. So they were closer than might appear on the surface.

"Giles knows he's going to lay low for a while. He has to tell her. He doesn't want her kicking up a fuss trying to find him. Or maybe he's confided in her already. That point doesn't matter. What does matter is the fact that she knew where he had gone, and why.

"So she lets it ride—until we show up. Then she begins to get the shimmies. She's suddenly dangerous. And somebody goes to her apartment to nullify the danger. The somebody knows that if she yells on her down trip, she'll be heard. There are too many people packed in that old building for her not to be heard.

"The somebody pops her on the noggin, rolls her out the window. And that's that."

The shudder hit Laura again. "The same person who raped and killed a little girl."

"Maybe. We don't know yet. We don't know for sure that Giles dropped out of sight because of Wally's trial. It might have been for some other reason. His past is spotted."

Laura pushed her food away for good. "Then we're right back where we started."

"Not quite. I'm simply saying we shouldn't draw only the conclusions we want to draw. We still have to find Giles."

"That's proving a little difficult, isn't it?"

"Only because we're not rolling yet. I'm going to need a thousand dollars."

"I can spare it."

"Good. It might buy us a door to Giles."

He was a round little man with a pleasant, chubby, very dark face. His teeth flashed like white fire when he smiled, which was often. He smoked the best Havana cigars, and they didn't cost him anything. A lot of his commodities cost Quinton nothing.

His office was in an old loft in Ybor City. It might have been the office of a loan shark. The furniture was old and scarred. The windows looked out on a drab, dirty alley. To get to the office, you had to go through an outer office where an expert in the hoodlum trade played at being secretary.

Nobody knew why Quinton remained in his old office. Maybe it was because he had started his career there with nothing more than an endless hunger for money, a trigger-quick brain and a fat body without a soul. Or maybe he kept the office because it made a deep cleavage between his personal and professional life. He lived in one of the best homes on the Bayshore. His wife was a boon to society editors. A girl had been beaten to death in one of Quinton's houses just last year, but his own daughters—he had two—were being educated in a convent.

To do business with Quinton you had to go to his office. His home was for social calls only.

Quinton knew how I felt about him, and I knew he regarded me as a dumb sucker. We let it lay like that, each knowing there'd never be any minor trouble between us. If anything ever caused us to buck each other, it would mean dirty trouble.

After we shook hands and he had seated himself behind his battered desk, I asked him how the waiters' and cigar-workers' unions were doing. He said they were doing all right. I didn't ask him about the houses. Quinton didn't own any houses. He simply collected off of that phase of life in Tampa.

We went through the whole rigmarole. He offered me a cigar, which I declined. Then a drink, which I turned down also. He didn't have a drink, either. He believed that only fools and weaklings messed with the stuff.

He folded his fat, short-fingered hands on his desk. "I see you're on the Tulman case, Ed."

"That's right."

"Sordid affair."

"Right again. But I don't think Tulman did it."

"Of course you don't. Giles Newell turn up yet? I saw in the papers that you're looking for him."

"Not yet."

"So you wondered if my waiters' union knows his whereabouts?"

"Something like that."

He popped his hands together in delight. He laughed.

A happy, little-boy laugh. He was as pleased as a kid on a quiz show. Or so it seemed.

While the laughter bubbled out of him, he said, "You want to scratch backs, Ed."

"That's right."

"How much?"

"A thousand dollars."

He shrugged. "Peanuts."

"There's money in peanuts, if you get enough of them."

"True. Anyhow, I wouldn't want payment for a favor. I'd accept it as a token."

"I don't care how you accept it, Quinton. Just give me Giles Newell's present address and I'll give you a thousand dollars."

"I don't have it at the moment, Ed."

"I can't wait too long, you know. Phone me, and I'll send the thousand by special messenger."

"I'll see what I can do," he said, standing up. He came around the desk, shook my hand, slapped me on the shoulder with his other hand.

I didn't like his touch. It made me think of the houses, and the venereal disease, and the long shifts the girls worked.

Quinton noted my reaction, but he was immune to it. It struck him as funny. He was still chuckling when I closed his office door behind me.

CHAPTER

12

I NEEDED to check the office and the telephone-answering service.

When I got to the office, I found Max the Giant waiting outside the door. He stood with the solid patience of a creature out of a Greek myth. He might have been there for minutes, or hours.

"Mrs. Wherry wants to see you," he said, without moving from the office door.

"All right," I said, getting out my keys.

"Mrs. Wherry wants to see you—now," he said.

He didn't intend to let me into my own office. He had a monorail brain, and Mrs. Wherry wanted to see me.

I looked him up and down. When I say up, I mean it. Compared to him, I was an undersized runt. I wasn't afraid of Max, but I had no yen to tangle with him. If I forced my way in and made a big issue out of a little one, it would be with the cold knowledge that I was going to get hurt. I could stand such a knowledge, if the price was right, but under the circumstances I decided the office could wait.

"Okay," I said.

"I have a car."

He waited for me to turn and go out of the building ahead of him. The car was the big, black limousine. It was parked near a fire plug, but it didn't have a ticket on it. It was an easily recognizable car.

"You ride up front with me," Max said.

We got in the car.

He started it, and it hissed away from the curb.

"What's on Mrs. Wherry's mind?" I asked.

"She'll tell you."

"You don't like me very much, hey, Max?"

"No. You're troubling Mrs. Wherry."

"Not intentionally."

"Your intentions don't matter to me. You just quit troubling Mrs. Wherry. She's got enough worries."

"I'll agree, but I've got a few worries of my own."

"I ain't interested," Max said, "in your worries. You just leave her alone, or I'll break your back."

He said it with mildness and simplicity.

We rode awhile in silence.

"I should have killed Tulman," he said finally. "Before the police came and arrested him. It would have settled a lot of things, including all the courtroom business and people like you. I could have killed him and closed it up once and for all and told the police that he was trying to get away and I killed him in the fight."

"Why didn't you?"

"She wouldn't let me. I think she wanted to. She knew all the mess that lay ahead, but she said we had to call the police instead."

"That was smart of her," I said.

"I don't think so. I believe Mr. Wherry would have done it the other way. Ruthie out there in the patio, and Tulman in our hands—I don't think Mr. Wherry would have hesitated. He'd have killed Tulman himself. Then called the police and said he'd ridded the world of a son-ofabitch."

"You miss the old man."

"Yes, I do. He understood. He hated people sometimes for the way they felt about the other people they called freaks. It wasn't pity he gave to us. Dammit, he understood!"

Max turned the Caddy into a palm-lined driveway. We passed through an open iron-grille gate. The driveway skirted a wide green lawn and wrapped itself around a white colonial-style house.

The house was an oddity for Florida, like an outlander who has come with all the earmarks of his northern clime and different way of living. You expected stables and good horses to go with a house like that.

Max and I got out of the car and went in the house. There was a high, long entry hall. A long living room opened off to my left. To my right was a sort of den. It must have been old Spicola Wherry's office. It held heavy leather furniture, a huge dark-colored desk. Pictures and streamers from a dead era in show business were all over the walls. Life-sized canvas paintings of freaks covered every inch of wall and ceiling space and gave the feeling that the freaks were about to run riot. The biggest painting was that of Max the Giant. Weather-stained from its years of service on the carnival circuits, it hung at the far end of the room. It showed Max dressed in a leopard skin, a glower on his face. His arms were cocked in a strong-man pose, his biceps flexed, breaking the chains that had been linked around his biceps.

"Mr. Rivers!"

I turned. The old lady was standing in the room across the hallway. She looked as solid and dogged as the freighters in Port Tampa.

"How do you do, Mrs. Wherry?"

"I do quite well," she growled as she walked toward me, "and you can save the amenities. Come into my office. I want to talk with you."

We went a few steps down the hall and turned into a small, cluttered room. It held a desk, two wooden chairs, a filing cabinet and a bookcase. It had the aspect of being a country lawyer's office. The bookcase was stacked with papers, not books. The chairs were well worn and old.

The desk held a litter of papers, a telephone and two Tampa telephone directories. One of the directories was the standard edition. The other was a yellow directory, a numerical index.

The old lady wedged herself behind the desk and sat down. Max the Giant stood breathing over my left shoulder.

Mrs. Wherry looked at me with blunt and bitter contempt. "At least," she said at last, "you're running true to form."

"Am I?"

"I knew you'd get around to naming a price."

There are times when you can learn more by keeping your mouth shut. So I kept my mouth shut.

She yanked open a desk drawer, took out a checkbook, and scribbled.

She ripped out the check and showed it to me. The check was for twenty-five-hundred dollars.

It was made payable to me.

I didn't reach for it, and she didn't hand it to me. She sat holding it and looking at me with those old, cold, contempt-filled eyes.

"Did you bring the stuff, Mr. Rivers?"

"No."

"Then you don't get the check."

"I see." I jerked my thumb over my shoulder. "Max was a little abrupt about bringing me here."

"You have the pictures in your office?"

"No."

She rose slowly. There was wrath and menace in every line of her strong old body. "I'll not be bamboozled—Mr. Bloxton."

"Aren't you getting the names mixed?"

"Bloxton, Rivers. They're one and the same."

"You sound pretty sure."

"I am sure, Bloxton-Rivers. Did you think to hide behind

a telephone? Did you think I couldn't trace you?" She dropped her eyes to the check. "You don't deserve this, you know. There's nothing lower than a creature who would trade on misery and scandal—especially when the victims have already borne too great an invasion of privacy. I should have you locked up, run out of Tampa for good. But I'm tired, Rivers. I'll take the easy way—this once. Don't think I will again. And don't think you'll get the money without surrendering the pictures."

"I seem to have lost the pictures, Mrs. Wherry." I was beginning to see light in the riddle. Somebody had put the blackmail touch on her, and she thought it was me.

"Then," she said regretfully, "we had best find them. Max!"

I turned in time to catch the judo chop on the base of my neck. My left side sagged in paralysis.

I reeled back and threw my right fist in his face. My knuckles glanced off his cheek. He located another nerve center, and I couldn't raise my arms.

Max raised his fist. I knew how big it must have looked to some of the bumpkin challengers who'd tried to lift old man Wherry's thousand bucks off the carny circuits.

The old lady was around the desk. She touched Max's arm and he stood rigid.

"Where are those pictures of Stephanie?" Mrs. Wherry said.

I drew my eyes from the expressionless seal's head and looked at her. Feeling, a dim ache, was coming back into my arms. I wouldn't let Max get away with that trick again.

I looked directly into the old girl's eyes. "I don't have any such pictures, Mrs. Wherry."

"Then you had no right to call and demand—"

"I didn't call you," I said.

She stood unmoving. Her gaze slipped my hair off, peeled back my scalp and examined every cell under my skull.

I didn't say anything more. She would either believe it, or she wouldn't.

She didn't want to believe it. If I were Bloxton, it would simplify things for her.

We stood that way for several seconds. Then, like pain, a doubt came to her eyes.

"I seem to have added fat to the fire," she said in a dismal voice.

"Referring to me? No, you haven't, Mrs. Wherry."

"Surely you'll use what I've told you—"

"To hold over you?" I said. "No. Not unless it concerns the guilt or innocence of Wallace Tulman."

"It has nothing to do with your client," she said bluntly.

"Then you don't have to be afraid of me, Mrs. Wherry. Do you think I've remained in business all these years by being untrustworthy?"

Our eyes met again. "I suspect," she said softly, "that one reason I dislike you, Mr. Rivers, is because you're very much like me."

"Maybe."

She moved away from Max. The giant relaxed. She made her way around her desk as if her feet were aching.

She stood with her hands on the desk, resting a moment. "I still want those pictures, Mr. Rivers. If you haven't got them, I've no earthly idea who might have. Will you work for me?"

"I've got a client."

"And you're looking for the man responsible for the pictures. I don't expect you to sell your client short, but you might keep a weather eye for the pictures. I'll pay you the amount that this Mr. Bloxton, whoever he is, demanded."

"If I find the pictures in the course of my work for Mrs. Tulman," I said, "I'll be glad to get them back in your hands."

"And no more publicity, Mr. Rivers. No more publicity at all."

"Not unless it will help Tulman."

"I see. That was your reason for those news stories?"

"In a hot climate, Mrs. Wherry, I don't spend any energy uselessly, if I can help it."

She sat down heavily. "You allay my fears, Mr. Rivers. Much as I dislike you, I'm beginning to feel I can trust you."

"You'll have to use your own judgment for that."

"Then find the pictures, and keep them quiet."

"I'll do what I can. I'll have to know what I'm looking for."

Shadows dropped over her face. "Nasty pictures, Mr. Rivers. Of my daughter."

"Who made them?"

"Giles Newell."

"What was the occasion?"

"Stephanie," she said, keeping her voice even and strong with an effort, "has always been consumed with anxieties and fears. At times these took an escape route through things of the flesh. Do you understand?"

"You make yourself clear," I said. "She seems to have considerable company in this day and time."

"Perhaps. I don't care about that. Let the world hang itself, if it will. I'm thinking of my daughter, her family, myself, my husband's memory."

"I would, too, in your shoes."

"You've got to understand that she wasn't promiscuous in the usual sense, Mr. Rivers. She didn't want to be. She hated herself for her weaknesses. But when the pressures built inside of her, she had to find excitement, forgetfulness of herself."

The old lady took a deep breath. "You must understand further, Mr. Rivers, that Giles Newell is an extremely handsome man. He affects an air of breeding and culture. It's real enough to fool a lot of people. He was eaten with the desire to put something real and substantial behind that veneer."

"You're going to get around to telling me that he and Stephanie had an affair."

"Yes, Mr. Rivers."

"You know," I said, "that you may be telling me the reason Giles Newell lied at the trial of Wallace Tulman."

Her face darkened. "Newell did not lie, Mr. Rivers. Contrary to what you think, in regard to Stephanie, Giles Newell had every reason to lie the other way. To lie Wallace Tulman to freedom."

"You're not getting home to me."

"Only because you won't let me tell this in my own way," she said shortly. "You think that because Giles and Stephanie had an affair Giles might have lied. Flimsy as all hell in the first place, Mr. Rivers! In the second, before the affair was over Stephanie despised Newell and he knew it. If he'd had a motive for lying that would have been it and such a motive would have led him to lie *for* Wallace Tulman, to strike back at Stephanie. Is that clear?"

"The mud's settling," I said. "Let's get back to the start of this affair. It wasn't her first?"

"I don't know," she said. "Perhaps it wasn't. She at least was careful and discreet. And she wasn't completely to blame."

"Milt Collins not a very good husband?"

"An excellent husband, except that he didn't understand Stephanie. Milt is cut out of more basic material. He likes to see ground break and buildings come up. He likes the feel of fresh-poured concrete under his feet. His music is the ringing of steel as a spike is being driven."

"A man's man."

"Yes. Or so he was. Now he isn't a hell of a lot of anything." She leaned back, closed her eyes. There was a fine sweat in the heavy caking of white powder on her forehead. She took a short breath. "Milt worked to amass money and retire young. He succeeded. In succeeding he failed, because he didn't know how to retire. He didn't know what to do with himself. So he drank. He might have gone back to work, but he'd convinced himself that he'd worked only to retire and that it was right that he retire. It was up to him now to make a success of retiring—but it's a battle he hasn't won.

"Stephanie could never become a part of such a man, Mr. Rivers. She loved the strength he'd possessed when they met. She felt a sense of duty toward him. She loved her children, more deeply than most women. She and Milt got along all right while he was working, building, planning. Perhaps it was because they didn't see much of each other, never got a chance really to know each other. He was the energetic, strong protector. Then they got to know each other, and he became just a man. A man deteriorating and going to waste. A restless man drowning his restlessness in drink. A man beginning to miss his own strength, seeing in her what he thought were weaknesses to be despised.

"Is it any wonder she was despairing and lonely?"

"I guess not," I said.

"Into this picture paint another figure, Mr. Rivers. Giles Newell. Debonair, understanding. He has some of the qualities of a chameleon. He adapts well. He senses the course of action, the tone of conversation he should take with a new acquaintance to be well liked.

"I think he believed he could wreck my daughter's marriage."

"And step in himself."

"Yes."

"But it didn't work," I said.

"She had a sense of duty, a loyalty. She could feel guilty quite easily. And she was not stupid, Mr. Rivers. She began to see that the water was getting deep. There was a last party. In Giles Newell's apartment. She was drinking—too much. He got the pictures then. I suppose he felt it was the last way he would ever get anything out of her."

"Maybe it was Giles who called you and posed as Mr. Bloxton."

"No. He didn't keep the pictures long. He tried to get some money from me, not long before that thing happened to little Ruthie and Wallace Tulman went to trial. I went to Newell's apartment to buy the pictures. They were gone. His regret and ire were genuine, Mr. Rivers. So real that he actually shed tears and accused Stephanie of slipping into the place and stealing them."

"So you didn't give him any money."

"Of course not. I left his apartment thinking he would never enter our lives again. But he did, of course—at the trial."

"You must have worried about the pictures."

"Certainly."

"Did you make an effort to find them?"

"I thought, until today, that Stephanie had them. I agreed with Newell's certainty of that."

"What did Stephanie say?"

"She didn't say anything, because I didn't ask her," the old lady said. She speared me with her eyes. "How do you go about asking a daughter if she had destroyed vulgar pictures she had stolen from the man who had taken them?"

"I see what you mean," I said.

"Then find those pictures!"

"I'll do what I can."

"Only Tulman comes first, Mr. Rivers?"

"Something like that."

"Tulman," she said. "Is there no end to the misery the vile little baby-face can bring into our lives?"

13

MAX THE GIANT drove me home. The old goddess he served might have edged toward my side of the fence, but Max still didn't like me. It was in his manner.

And the feeling was mutual.

I thanked him curtly, got out of the car and went up to my apartment.

I opened the door.

"Hi, Ed," Evie Grove called from the kitchen.

"Make yourself at home," I said.

"Thanks."

"Janitor let you in?"

"That's right. Do you like bacon and eggs?"

"I can eat them." I went into the kitchenette. She was cooking bacon on the gas burner. I opened the ice box, got out a cold beer, put a hole in the top of the can and drank half of it.

Her blond hair was loose about her face. Her cheeks were flushed from the heat. She gave me a smile. "I got tired of artificiality, Ed."

"Is that right?"

"So I came to see you."

"That's nice. Been here long?"

"Oh, not long."

"You're lying, Evie."

She gave me a quick look. "Why do you say that, you darling bear?"

"You made a call from my phone."

"Well, really ..."

"I don't like for people to use my phone for that kind of call, Evie."

"I don't know what you're talking about!"

"You called Mrs. Wherry. You muffled your voice and said you were a Mr. Bloxton. Where'd you ask her to leave the money and pick up the pictures?"

Evie stood with the spatula in her hand. She put it down. She moved to me and slipped her arms about my waist. Face tilted back, she smiled at me.

"What a delightful little tale, darling!"

I could feel the sleek, warm length of her body against mine. She could feel it too. Her eyes got embers in their depths.

"It's no dice, Evie."

"No?" she said softly.

"No."

She whispered a laugh and kissed me. Then her lips grew cool. She pulled her face back and now her eyes were angry.

"Something wrong with me, Ed?"

"Nope."

"Then—it's somebody else. Who, big bear?"

"Quit trying to sidetrack the issue."

"Your client? The elegant and proper Laura Tulman?" Her feminine instinct ran deep. Predatory. Sharp. Her eyes glinted. "So help me, that's it! Do you know, many men would have liked to make a pass at her?"

"Stow it, Evie." I disengaged her arms and pushed her back. She stood on a precipice for a moment. Then her face cooled and she smiled as if finding humor in the thought of Laura Tulman. I was glad she'd decided to laugh it off.

"You won't get to first base, dear bear," she said.

"We were talking about pictures," I said.

"I don't know anything more than I did a moment ago." She turned back to the bacon.

I gripped her arm and turned her toward me. "Calling from here might have seemed a brilliant trick to you, Evie. But actually it was dumb. The old lady had the call traced. She looked it up in a yellow numerical phone book. My phone. So the call had to come from here. See?"

"Let me go!"

I let her go. She stood holding her arm. The bacon was beginning to scorch.

"Old lady Wherry reached the obvious conclusion. That Mr. Bloxton was me. She didn't go for this rendezvous stuff. She's more direct. She had Max the Giant pick me up."

Evie's eyes went wide.

"She wants those pictures, Evie," I said. "Bad. She offered to pay me for them."

"So that's it!"

"No, that isn't it," I said shortly. "Tulman comes first. I told her that. But I also told her that I'd hand over the pictures if they turned up."

"Then you could split with me, Ed, if the money doesn't mean anything to you."

"I didn't say it didn't mean anything. I only said that a first client remains first, regardless of how much more money somebody else can pay."

"Well, I haven't got the pictures!"

"Oh, hell, Evie, let's cut out the ring-around-a-rosy."

The bacon was burning, but good. I reached out and flipped the flame off.

Evie's face shadowed with self-pity. "You just ride rough-shod over everything! Why shouldn't the old lady pay? She's got more than plenty."

"That still isn't the point. The guy with a dime may

think the guy with ten bucks has got more than plenty, but the guy with the tenner might not agree."

"You try to mix me up, Ed! But I still think I ougĥt to have something. I have to live by the skin of my teeth and those damn Wherrys and Collinses have got everything."

"Yeah," I said, "a dead little girl, a young woman in the crazy house."

"Oh, that"—Evie shrugged—"that could happen to anybody. They've still got all the money in the world." She sank down in a chair, a rickety old chair at the rickety old table, and for a moment I thought she was going to cry. "Please, Ed. Don't just take the pictures from me. They're all I got left to raise a few bucks on."

"You must have accumulated some clothes and jewels the last few years."

"I have to have my clothes, Ed, and I couldn't bear to part with my jewels."

"Okay, Evie," I said, "I'll be very unkind to you. I'll take a day's pay and you can keep the rest."

Her eyes lighted. "Why, thanks, darling bear!" She jumped to her feet, put her arms around me and kissed me on the lips.

She drew back her face, her eyes cautious suddenly. "What do you mean by saying you're being unkind to me?"

"You'll understand in due time."

"That sounds a little like an insult, Ed."

"No, just a word of prophecy. The longer you skin through the tougher it will be when there's no more skinning to do. Don't ever look down, Evie. It's a deep, dark hole on either side of that tightrope—and one of these days the rope is bound to break."

Her face was deeply troubled for a moment. Then she forced some humor in her eyes. "Puritan," she said. "Just a plain old Puritan."

"That's right, feeling sorry for you."

"You don't have to do that, Ed! I don't like pity."

"Let's skip it. Where are the pictures?"

"Dammit, I don't want your pity!"

"All right," I shouted. "So the hell with you."

"Don't be so mean to me, Ed. I like you a lot. Can't you see the feeling I want from you?"

"And I want those pictures. "

She jerked away from me and flounced into the bed-sitting room. "The lousy pictures are in my cottage. If that's all you can think about, we'll go get them."

"That's better," I said.

The cottage was a love nest, but not the sticky kind. It held an air of comfort, of perfumed privacy. The thick rugs and heavy drapes softened all sound. The living-room bar held a collection of crystal and amber bottles. The world seemed a long way off.

"Like my place?" Evie asked.

"Yeah. Where you got the pictures?"

"Can't you get your mind off work for a minute?" She swished into the bedroom, adding over her shoulder, "Help yourself to a drink."

I didn't want one.

She wasn't in the bedroom long. She came back carrying a five-by-seven manila envelope.

I opened the envelope and slid the pictures out. There were half a dozen of them. All of Stephanie Collins. Not nice.

Backing the prints were the negatives.

Evie watched me with her head tilted to one side. "That's it, the whole package. Okay?"

"Unless there are other prints drifting around."

"If there are, Giles made them."

"Before you snitched the package?"

"That's right. But I'm sure he made only the one set of prints before I got the package from his apartment."

"He isn't going to like this," I said.

"Oh, I can handle Giles—if we ever catch up with him."

The door buzzer sounded, discreet and subdued. I slid the package inside my coat pocket. A caller would give me a good chance to get away and return the package to old lady Wherry.

Evie clicked the latch on the door. Somebody outside hit the house with a bulldozer. The door flew open and knocked her sprawling against me. She grabbed me to keep from falling.

Over her shoulder I saw Garcia.

He was flanked by two hefty plain-clothes cops.

Garcia looked at me and licked his lips. I saw a caged panther lick his lips like that once.

C H A P T E R

14

"Please, Rivers," Garcia said softly, "just make one phony move."

"No, thanks," I said.

Evie disentangled herself from me. She pushed her mane of blond hair from her face. Her eyes were wide. I couldn't tell whether it was from fear or excitement.

Garcia and his pals formed a half-moon around me.

"I thought you were taking a forced vacation," I said.

"I got tired of loafing."

"You got tired mighty fast," I said.

"It just goes to show you how quick the heat can cool in this town. You're a pretty dumb boy, Ed. You been around long enough to know the ropes."

"Yeah," I said.

"Search him," Garcia told his boys.

"Now wait a minute . . ." Evie said.

"We'll get to you, sister. Or you want to spend ninety days in jail?"

Evie backed away until the edge of a heavy divan struck the backs of her legs.

"You can't do this," she said. "I have friends."

"You had friends," Garcia said, "until you started chumming with this cluck."

The two cops on either side of me reached to search me.

"You got a warrant?" I asked Garcia.

He laughed.

One of the cops got my knee in his groin. The other rushed to meet my right fist with his nose. He grabbed his nose, howled and went back.

Garcia stepped in. His fists gleamed dully. The brass knucks cracked against my temple.

The room expanded with sudden speed. I saw the carpet coming.

I heard Garcia laugh again.

He kicked me in the belly.

"Search him, boys," he said quietly.

In the distance, I could hear Evie weeping. She was begging them to lay off. She hadn't done a thing. I was just a guy she'd met and invited in for a drink.

Garcia told her to shut up and the quietness of his voice had a smothering effect on her.

Garcia emptied my pockets. I pulled myself to a chair and crawled into it. My head hurt and my stomach was jerking as I watched him examine my stuff.

He sucked in his breath when he saw the pictures of Stephanie Collins.

He shifted his gaze from the pictures to me, his eyes dancing with pleasure.

"Extortion," he said.

"Nope," I said, holding my stomach, "just doing a chore."

"We'll see who believes that, Rivers. You were pretty big and smart, weren't you? Thought you'd dumped me, didn't you? Now we'll see. Brother, we'll really see."

I kept my mouth shut and at Garcia's gesture I got to my feet.

Evie stood with her hands clasped tight in front of her. She couldn't take her eyes off those pictures, which Garcia was holding. She watched as he slipped them into the side pocket of his tropical-weight coat. She bit her lip and I thought she was going to break out crying. She had to look away when Garcia patted the pictures snug in his pocket.

Garcia gave her a glance. "You stick around, sister. We might want to talk to you."

Her shoulders shivered faintly. She kept her back to Garcia. She was really taking the loss of those pictures hard.

Garcia gave me a shove. "Get going, smart boy."

Julian Patrick was in his office when we reached headquarters. I figured he'd been summoned from his home by telephone.

Julie rocked gently in the swivel chair behind his desk as Garcia followed me into the office and heeled the door closed.

"This had better be good," Julie said.

"It is, chief," Garcia said. "My idea panned out with a real nice surprise." He gave me a sidelong look and grin of unholy pleasure as he moved around and dropped the manila envelope on Patrick's desk.

Patrick leaned forward and opened the envelope. He glanced at the contents and went absolutely rigid. He paled slightly.

"Where'd you get these?"

"Off Rivers," Garcia said.

"Where'd he get them?"

"Off the chick, I guess."

"Any idea where she got them?"

Garcia shrugged.

Patrick nailed his glance on me. "Want to open up, Ed?"

"There's nothing to open up about."

"I believe there is. Ed, there's one thing you ought to get straight. You're not dealing with an Ybor City *bolita* ring. You're trying to befoul one of the oldest families in Tampa. We don't like that, Ed."

"I'm sorry about that, Julie."

"I wish you really were. The department wants no trouble."

"I don't either."

"But you seem determined to make it. Can't you understand the whole tragedy was explained, wrapped up, put away. Why do you want to hurt these people further?"

"I don't."

"But that's what you're doing. You must have a reason. Tell me, Ed. I'm aching to know the reason."

"I think Wallace Tulman is innocent," I said. "I think he's an innocent, bewildered child in a man's body about to pay for something he didn't do."

"Oh, you do?" Patrick said with briny frost in his voice. "You think that—so it doesn't matter that all the machinery of organized law, legal procedure, trial by jury, guarantees of his civil rights were followed to the letter, only to prove him guilty."

"Juries can be wrong, Julie."

"And I guess you can't?"

"I'm not often wrong, Julie. Can you ever remember me being wrong? I don't like to be wrong. It doesn't pay. I'm not wrong, because unlike your juries I don't presume a man innocent until he's blackened and smeared into looking guilty. I start out thinking he's guilty as hell until something happens to make me think otherwise."

"You're talking big, Ed."

"I'm just telling you," I said.

"You need proof to back up that kind of talk."

"I didn't want this case, Julie. Until somebody got so damned scared I was going to take it that he tried to knock my brains out right in my own apartment building."

"Oh, that," Julie tried to pass it off with a wave of his hand.

"Yes, that. And a law-enforcement agency that's locked up its mind and thrown the key away. And a drunken woman who falls out of a slum apartment building all the way to the alley below without making a sound. You want me to keep talking, Julie?"

"I want you to quit moving like an elephant in a flower garden."

"I haven't found the flowers yet, Julie, only the weeds."

"Including these, I suppose," he said, laying his hand on the pictures.

"They're weedy enough."

"Valuable, too."

"You charging me with extortion?"

"I might."

"You better talk to the old girl first. She asked me to get the pictures."

"When?"

"This afternoon."

"Why'd she pick you for the job? She hates your guts for lighting a fire under a pot that had simmered down."

"She thought I had the pictures."

"She get a call, or something like that?"

"Could be," I said.

"Blackmail demand?"

"Maybe."

Patrick rocked back in his chair. "You're not doing so good, Ed."

"No?"

"No. She gets a blackmail demand. She contacts you— making it obvious she thought the call had come from you. She asks you to get the pictures. And—surprise—what do you know, a few hours later you've got them. A lot of people would read into that nothing but plain extortion. You fell off the end of the pier with this bit of fishing, Ed."

"I don't think so," I said. "I didn't have the pictures when Mrs. Wherry called me. I got them from Evie Grove. You asked a minute ago where she got them. I'll tell you. From Giles Newell."

"So?"

"So maybe you'd like for the papers to know that the state's star witness against Wallace Tulman was going around with a mittful of naughty pictures of the dead little girl's mother."

The office got very quiet.

Beside me, after a moment, I could hear Garcia breathing heavily.

Patrick simply sat and looked at me.

"We must never lose sight of one cold fact," I said. "A creep got hold of a little girl named Ruthie Collins. If it wasn't Tulman, it had to be somebody else, with some strangely disordered gray matter in his skull. So, in view of his actions and these pictures, I'm beginning to wonder more and more who and what Giles Newell really is."

"That your hole card, Ed?" Patrick said.

"I've played worse hands."

"You always like to have a hole card. But this time it's a joker—and the joker isn't wild. I used a pair of tweezers on Newell's life, public and private. I had a hole card of my own. I was prepared to counter any move the defense might make to discredit the witness on whom our whole case depended. I can tell you definitely, Ed, that Giles Newell was behind the bar in the Yacht Club the entire evening of the little girl's murder."

Patrick rose and came around the desk. "Lock him up, Garcia."

"On what charge?" I asked.

"I can hold you on an open charge for twenty-four hours,"

Patrick said. "In that time I may be able to show Mrs. Tulman the hopelessness and sheer nonsense of what she's instigated."

"Come on." Garcia leered at me.

"Keep your hands off," I said. "Julie, you're making a mistake."

"I'll take a chance," Patrick said.

"You can't bluff us this time, Rivers," Garcia said. "I guess the papers will give me a different break now."

"There'll be nothing in the papers from you," Patrick told him.

"Aw, chief, something to counteract—"

"You talk to a single reporter," Patrick said, "and I'll see your next retirement is permanent. Now get Rivers out of here."

I preceded Garcia out of the office. At the doorway, I stopped. "Do I get a lawyer?"

"You're incommunicado for twenty-four hours, old friend," Patrick said mildly. He crossed the office and closed the door in my face.

Garcia chuckled as he took me down to the desk, booked me and sent me upstairs with a couple of cops in uniform.

They gave me a private cell, and I stood at the window looking through the bars at what I could see of Tampa.

Patrick was in a position to mount a real assault on Laura's intention and determination. Tulman was still the patsy, and there seemed less that could be done about it than there had been two or three days ago.

The trial, imprisonment, the prospect of death in the electric chair, had put a lot of uncertainty in Wallace Tulman. Now let a mild-speaking official visit him, tell him of failure, give him that extra nudge. Could be that the confusion would clear from Tulman's mind. He might decide once and for all that he was guilty, no questions remaining. He might communicate that message to her, asking her to call off the whole thing.

Patrick was capable of arranging it.

I tried to keep myself from thinking it, but the thought was there:

If Patrick arranged it, she would be free.

CHAPTER

15

I HAD a breakfast of hominy grits and sausage. From the looks of the early sun outside, the day was going to be a scorcher. My flesh was heavy with the heat, dull with sweat. I brushed my pants with my hands and shook out my light seersucker coat. It didn't help. The suit was a wrinkled, sweat-stained, heat-tormented rag.

I got the loan of a razor. The jailer stood by while I shaved. He gnawed some conversation, but I didn't talk back, and finally he gave up.

I sat alone until almost noon.

At that time, the jailer came back to the cell and said, "You got company."

"Well, show him in."

"He's on his way."

The jailer walked down a steel-lined corridor, clanging a couple of steel-barred doors behind him.

At the end of the corridor, the elevator indicator arrow swung to a stop. The lift opened and a man got out. The jailer clanged the doors again, bringing the man back to my cell.

The caller was Milt Collins. His big, softening face was pale. There were pouches under his eyes, and his eyeballs were laced with red threads. He looked a little disheveled, and more than tired.

But he was sober. Painfully, coldly sober. He still wore an invisible mantle of power and ego, exuding a feeling that it was his natural right to boss men. But he carried another little air about him today. Maybe it was a touch of indecision and humility.

He had his panama hat in his hand, and the big, blunt fingers opened and closed on the brim of the hat.

"Hello, Rivers." He stood at the cell door, looking between the bars at me.

"What's on your mind?" I asked.

"I came over to get you out of here."

I didn't say anything.

After a minute, he said, "You want out, don't you?"

"I dunno."

His face pinked. "What the devil do you mean? Any man would want out."

"I don't figure to be in long."

"You might have some surprises in store for you. Patrick could build a strong case of extortion against you. That would mean about twenty years."

"I'd be an old man when I got out."

His jaw made like a heavy-set steel trap. "This isn't a joking matter, Rivers. I'm not so sure you didn't have the pictures the whole time."

"Then why are you here?"

He let go a breath. He was a man eaten inside and for a moment I had a glimpse of what it was like to live in his house, his body, his skull.

"Okay," he said, "I came to ask a favor."

"Well, why didn't you?"

He passed a big capable-looking hand through his hair. "Because I'm me, I guess. I like to give the orders, the favors."

"It could work both ways."

He raised his eyes. His gaze was steady, held that way with an effort. "Keep it out of the papers," he begged.

"And you'll spring me right now?"

"Yes."

"It'll have to go further than that."

"There's a limit to what I can do."

"This had better not be beyond the limit," I said. "If I keep mum, Patrick's department has got to do the same. I'm not going to have Garcia pictured as the brave and honest detective, framed by a shady shamus, who on his own time put said shamus in the clink."

"Surely, it wouldn't matter—"

"It does matter. I'll tell you something. You don't have to live in the Estates to worry about your reputation."

"Of course not," he said quickly. "If I sounded a little snobbish, I'm sorry, Rivers."

"Well, that's it. My rep in a way is worth more to me than yours to you. My rep is part of my living—and I'll fight back to keep it intact. You'd better tell Patrick that."

"I'm sure Patrick will understand."

"Okay. Get your high-priced lawyer ready."

"He's already at work. In Patrick's office. I—we got the pictures, Rivers. Thanks."

"Patrick turn them over to you?"

Milt Collins nodded.

"I worked to get them back," I said. "I landed in the clink to get them back."

"You'll be paid."

"I want two days' pay. The rest I promised to the young lady I got the pictures from. Evie Grove. Know her?"

"I've met her."

"Friend?"

"To a certain extent. She was around the club a lot. Sometimes she rounded out a party."

"She worked with Giles Newell."

"Most people around the club knew that."

"Did you know there was anything between Giles and your wife?" I asked.

"I don't like a direct question of that nature, Rivers."

"And I don't like to ask them. That makes us even. But if you don't answer, I might think the worst."

His eyes slid over me. "Damn you," he said. "I find myself liking some of your qualities, Rivers."

"That's fine."

"To answer your question, I didn't know there was anything between Stephanie and Giles. I assure you that the pictures shocked me more than anybody else. I didn't know her discontentment was running so deep."

"A man sometimes finds he doesn't know a lot of things that were under his nose."

"Yes, he does," Collins said, and there was a note of real humility in his voice. It was almost shocking, coming from him.

"I guess you hate Giles," I said.

"Isn't it a little late for that?"

"Do you know where he is?"

"No."

"Do you want to find out?"

"I said," his voice got harsh, "that it seems a little late for all that. What are you driving at, Rivers?"

"I was wondering," I said, "if you had run him to cover."

"Meaning?"

"If a man like you found out about his wife and Newell, I wouldn't be surprised to learn that an explosion had taken place."

He studied me for a moment. We were standing close together, only the cell door separating us.

"There might have been an explosion," he said. "I guess I would have killed the sonofabitch."

"I guess you would have."

"But I didn't—because I didn't know. I've told you the truth."

"There had to be a reason for him pulling the Houdini."

"I think you're attaching too much importance to his vanishing act."

"I like to know the whys and wherefores," I said.

"It seems very simple. After the trial, he simply decided to drop out of sight and recover from the strain."

"How about his job?"

"It was either resign or work out a notice from the club. Remember that he'd been the star witness in a sensational trial. He would attract attention. Drunks would quiz him for details. The club couldn't use him any longer."

"Ordway didn't tell me that."

"Ordway is a very discreet club manager," Milt Collins said.

"So there were other jobs."

"Not in the sort of places where Giles wanted to work. No, his disappearance was a perfectly natural thing, Rivers."

Milt Collins took his leave. Thirty minutes later, Julian Patrick came up to see me.

"How you feeling, Ed?"

"Okay."

"Sensible?"

"That depends."

"We're going to let you out of here."

"How nice. Good thing I knew the dope on those pictures or I'd have rotted in here."

"It's a thought. You won't have the pictures next time— if there is a next time."

"There won't be, Julie."

"That's what I like to hear. When my friends have to walk tightropes I like to see them keep their balance."

"I'll be careful," I said.

"You'd better be good," Julie said. He nodded to the jailer. The big bohunk put a key in the lock and turned it.

I walked out of the cell. Patrick and I rode the elevator down without speaking.

In the downstairs corridor, Patrick turned in one direction and I went in the other.

Evie Grove was waiting for me outside the building. She looked willowy and sleek in a summery print dress, her blond hair loose about her face.

"Well," she sighed in relief, "I thought they'd changed their minds and were going to leave you in the dungeon for mouse bait."

She linked her arm in mine while I stood on the curb and flagged a cab.

"Ed," she said, "I hate to bring up business—"

"You'll be hearing from the Wherrys," I said. "They've got the pictures. They'll honor their commitment."

"Thanks, Ed."

A cab swung to the curb and stopped. I opened the door, and Evie Grove got in. I closed the door.

She looked at me out of the window. "Aren't you going with me, Ed?"

"You don't need me for this errand. Just go someplace and phone the Wherrys."

I turned and walked away.

I went up to the office. It shimmered with a dry, heavy heat. I opened the windows, got a couple of fresh handkerchiefs out of a desk drawer, mopped some sweat off my face and neck.

Then I sat down behind the desk and thought about the whole thing. I thought of each person involved, and each incident, and each word that had been said, and each inflection with which it had been said.

I'd never seen little Ruthie Collins, but I thought about her, too. About her short, lonely life. About the moment of terror she had known.

I'd told Milt Collins that a man doesn't know things that are right under his nose sometimes.

I was nagged with the feeling that the whole thing was right under my nose.

But I couldn't pin it down.

I reached for the phone and dialed Laura's number.

She answered as if she'd been sitting with her hand hovering over the phone.

"Ed."

"Where are you?" she asked.

"At my office. You know I've been in the jug?"

"Milt Collins told me."

"Did he tell you why I was there?"

"No."

"I'll explain the whole thing later."

"You're all right?"

"Yes," I said. I wanted to hold onto the feeling the concern in her voice gave me.

"Ed?"

"Yes?"

"I'm tying a knot in the end of my rope just to hold on. Couldn't we take the rest of the day off? Go to the beach. Just rest a few hours? We've been so close to it."

"Sure," I said. "I'll check the morgue—"

"I did that this morning, Ed. The Hofstetter woman is still there. Giles hasn't shown up to claim his sister's body yet."

"I'll be over in about an hour," I said.

She was wearing a simple white dress, white sandals, a coil of white scarf in her hair. It was the right contrast for her dark coloring.

Her eyes were large and deep in her face, luminous with strain. She was right. She needed a little rest; she had to forget it for a little while. But she looked more beautiful than ever.

Her bare legs flashed as she preceded me across the living area. Beyond the glass doors that shut out the patio, a brassy hot sky was gathering a few clouds. The air was forming a faint vacuum within itself.

"We might get a squall," I said.

"Do you mind?" she smiled over her shoulder.

"I'd welcome anything to break the heat," I said.

"I've got sandwiches and a couple of thermos bottles all packed."

"I've got a rented car out front," I said. "Where'll we go?"

"I don't care, Ed. Just take me someplace."

I carried the basket of food and towels and beach blanket out to the car. We got in, and I drove for nearly an hour. Out of Tampa on a main highway, off on a state road, off on a shell-surfaced road north of Clearwater.

We jounced between thickets of palmetto, cabbage palm and scrub pine. The heat was a quivering, a humming, the faint song of the dry, rustling wilderness.

Then we rounded a bend, and there was the Gulf, and a mile of pure white beach. The sun crowned the blue-green wavelets with jewels. Not a house was in sight, or a boat, or a single other human being. Everything was as untouched and unspoiled as it had been before the advent of the first man.

Laura got out of the car and stood looking down the half-moon of beach, the water, the tangle of mangrove on the landward side.

I hefted the picnic and swimming stuff out of the car and carried them down the beach.

"Old haunt of yours, Ed?" she chided with a smile.

"I've never been here before," I said. "I didn't know where that cow-trail excuse for a road ran. I only felt that I had to be lucky today."

"Turn around," she said.

I turned around and stood that way for a few moments.

"Okay," she said.

She had unbuttoned the white dress, slipped it off and

dropped it on the blanket. She stood slender and firm in a white bathing suit. She tucked her hair under a bathing cap, raced to the water and plunged in, a tan-and-silver arrow.

I watched her break the surface and start swimming out as I shucked the clothes I was wearing over my bathing trunks.

We swam a good mile out; then I saw the squall moving in. It was still a great distance out in the endless Gulf, but already the water around us stirred as if it held a muffled growl.

We swam in without haste, threw towels around our shoulders, and carried our picnic stuff back of the beach to a giant banyan tree. The tree looked a million years old. It dropped roots in a tangle from its heavy lower branches. The roots, ranging in size from threads to massive supports as big around as barrels, formed a shadowed maze.

We spread the blanket and set the basket in a little place under the vast old tree where pine needles had been carried in by the breeze and accumulated.

Laura sat down, legs crossed and stretched before her. I dropped beside her. She looked fresh and vital, drops of water standing on her face and shoulders. She took off her cap and shook out her hair.

I laid my hand on her shoulder. I felt a faint spasm go through her muscle. A rising breeze from the Gulf brushed the hair from her face.

I kissed her. Not as I'd kissed any of the occasional women who'd dotted the lonely stretch of years. I kissed her the way I'd once kissed a girl many years ago who I'd believed to be good as well as beautiful. There had been innocence in my world in those long-ago, lost years.

I felt her lips come to life. Her hand trailed fire across my back. Her arms grew tight, and the heat and hunger in her lips were the heat and hunger of a female animal.

She began crying.

I raised my head and she put her hands over her face while the sobs ripped out of her.

"Ed . . ." Her voice sounded far away.

"You don't have to explain. It's him, isn't it? Tulman?"

"Yes."

"You don't love him."

"Not like this. I didn't know it could be so savage as this. But he's my husband."

A pulse was pounding in my temples and I was having trouble breathing. My fingers dug into the sand until it felt as if the nails were tearing loose.

Then I looked at the suffering of her.

"It's okay," I said. "It's all right."

"I'm sorry, Ed. I thought . . . I wanted . . ."

"I know. We'd better get back."

We got up, knocked some of the sand off ourselves. I picked up the picnic basket. She gathered the towels and blanket.

Silently, we walked back to the car. The sky was darkening. From the distance came the growl of thunder. The wind was stiffer, blowing in the first fat drops of rain. The drops hit the beach with angry weight.

We slipped our clothes over our swimming things and got in the car.

I stepped on the starter. The motor turned over but failed to start.

I kept it up until the battery was almost down.

16

WHEN I got out of the car and opened the hood, I didn't spot the trouble right away. I'm not much of a mechanic, and the distributor and wiring looked all right to me.

I checked the gas line. The trouble was there. The rubber line leading from the fuel pump to the carburetor was swollen and puffy with age. It had sprung a rip on its lower side, separating the engine from its gas supply.

I tried wrapping a strip of towel around the line, but it didn't work. The toweling admitted too much air.

Finally I leaned against the window of the car. "Looks like I'll have to walk back to the main road and get some help," I said.

"Want company?"

I looked at the nearing squall. The sky was a nasty gray, and the front was moving in fast. The rain was steadying out, becoming more than isolated drops.

"It's less than half a mile," I said, "and I think we passed a filling station on the main road not too far down. You'll be more comfortable in the car. It won't take me long."

She nodded, and I turned away from the car. I plodded through the yielding sand to the state road. A wicked flare of lightning cut through the massing clouds. Kettledrums of thunder crashed against earth and sky.

As if the thunder had been a signal, the clouds opened.

The rain came with a rush. A tiny part of it turned to steam in the heat, forming a veil like fog.

I didn't mind the wetting. It was cooling. I started down the highway, squinting into the rain. The clouds made war overhead, throwing big bombs of lightning. .

Then a brief stillness came, as is the nature of such squalls. The wind held. The lightning held until more static electricity could build up. The last volley of thunder rolled to silence.

I heard the whine of the car's engine. My first thought was that I might get a lift.

He was coming fast behind me, when I turned. I jerked up my thumb.

And in the length of time it took me to lift my hand I realized something was wrong.

The accelerator of the light, black car was down to the floor. The car was coming right at me. The grillwork was a hungry mouth.

. I stopped breathing. I almost stopped living. I moved, without willing myself to move.

I guess my face carried a nightmarish expression. My mouth was open in a silent scream.

The right front fender of the car grazed the waistband of my pants. The contact between metal and my flesh was barely made. Even so, I felt as if a sledge hammer had hit me in the side.

An invisible rope jerked me off my feet and hurled me off the highway.

I pinwheeled for about twenty feet, landing on my back, feeling nothing for a moment.

Then the rain stung my face. I'd crashed in swampy palmetto, and I pulled myself around in the muck and started crawling away.

I heard the car slow. Then I heard the steady chug of a diesel engine. A tractor and trailer was moving down the highway.

I was shaking all over. I kept moving, bellying along through the palmetto.

I don't know whether or not the black car stopped. Maybe whoever was in it came back to see if he'd finished the job. Maybe the passing truck scared him off.

In any event, he couldn't afford to be conspicuous. He couldn't risk a passing car seeing his car parked, seeing him prowling a palmetto thicket beside the highway.

So he didn't have time to find me.

I eeled out of the palmetto onto the sandy beach road and lay there a moment getting some strength back. It was good to breathe, to feel the sand beneath me. The rain smelled sweet. If he'd found me in the palmetto, I wouldn't have had the strength to raise a finger to save myself.

I got my feet under me and felt my side. The numbness was going away. I was going to have a sore rib cage for a week or ten days, but I couldn't feel anything broken.

Favoring the side, I limped back to the rented car on the beach.

Laura was smoking a cigarette and looking at the stormy reaches of the Gulf. She had the windows of the car down. She heard the sound of my footstep as my shoe crushed a shell.

She looked around quickly. Her eyes went wide. "Ed!"

I moved to the car and leaned against it.

She got out. "I didn't expect you back so quickly. Your face—it's so gray!"

"Somebody in a car tried to flatten me on the state road."

"Oh, Ed . . ."

"Must have followed us. Slipped in here while we were swimming and gimmicked the gas line. Then went back to his car and waited in the shelter of the pines, off the shoulder, for the target to come walking out."

She lifted the back of her hand to her cheek and stood staring at me. The rain plastered wisps of her hair about her cheeks, beat unnoticed against her face.

I pulled myself around and opened the hood of the car. I jerked the rubber fuel-pump-to-carburetor line all the way out.

The line left black, greasy marks on my hands. I turned the line over. The rip in it had been hacked there by a knife. The cords woven into the line showed clean where they had been cut.

The squall was moving on inland. The rain slackened, the earth began to steam.

I dropped the line in my pocket.

Laura was standing perfectly still beside the car.

"Do you want to quit, Ed?"

"Do you want me to?"

"I don't think that's the question. It's your life that's in danger. I won't blame you, if you decide to quit."

I put my hand on her bare arm. My fingers curled around the flesh. Then I eased my grip. "I don't think you understand me very well."

"Yes, I do."

"Then why'd you ask me that?"

"I thought it was proper."

"Okay, so you've asked me," I said. "Let's go get a replacement for this line. This time you're walking with me. I don't want you on a deserted beach with a character like that around."

As we started toward the state road, my right leg dragged a little. But there was nothing wrong with my right hand.

It rested in my pants pockets.

So did the .38.

If he was still out there, he'd find the target fighting back.

17

It was almost two miles to the country-store filling-station. The highway was as peaceful as a Sunday afternoon. The sun was bright and hot again. Tendrils of steam rose from the black surface of the road. The day was muggier than ever.

The outpost of civilization was a rambling building of weathered clapboards sheltered by some huge and beautiful willow trees. There was a single gas pump out front. The building was decorated with tin signs, in various states of decay and rust, advertising Coca-Cola and Bruton's snuff. A redbone hound dog crawled from under the building and came snuffling toward us.

"Howdy."

A tall, rawboned old geezer stood in the doorway of the store. Age had dried him out, but it hadn't sapped him.

He squirted tobacco juice in the yard, wiped his mouth, looked me up and down.

"Have an accident?"

"Yeah," I said. "Got a replacement part for this?"

He stepped into the store yard and I handed him the gashed line.

He hmmmmmmed over it. "Reckon I might have."

I followed him around the building. He owned a considerable junk pile, some of it in boxes. He scratched around in a wooden barrel for a few minutes.

"Here you are, friend," he said. "That'll be a dollar."

I paid the old man and asked him if he'd seen the black car. Or the diesel rig. Maybe if I could identify the rig, the driver could tell me something about the black car that had been just ahead of him.

It was a long chance, and I didn't expect anything from it.

I got exactly what I expected. The old man had seen neither. He'd been napping on a cot in his store.

I left Laura at the old man's place, walked back to the rented car, and installed the second-hand gas line.

We ate the picnic sandwiches as we drove back to town.

When I dropped Laura and went to my apartment, I stripped down, ran a tub of cool water and got cleaned up. My right side was settling purple. It was tender. It would stiffen up some, but it would take something more to keep me from moving around.

I put on a short-sleeved cotton sport shirt and a well-worn Palm Beach suit. Then I went out in the kitchenette and turned on the fan. I sat in front of it while I drank a quart of icy beer.

I thought of the way that car had looked coming at me. Like a thing alive. I shivered faintly, thinking how close I'd come to being a statistic in the accident column.

The car meant desperation.

Desperation meant I was getting close.

Still, I didn't know what I was close to.

And if I was that close, I'd have to watch my step.

Patrick had said I might get killed, and Patrick could be so right.

It wasn't just a case any longer. I guess I knew it from the first. It was a fight for survival, and I could avoid it only by letting Wallace Tulman die.

The phone rang.

I got up, went in the other room and picked the phone up.

I said hello.

A smooth, well-modulated voice said, "Is this Ed Rivers speaking?"

"That's right."

"I understand you've been wanting to see me."

The muggy heat prickled me. "That depends on who you are."

"Giles Newell."

"Where are you?"

"In town. I've just made arrangements for my sister's cremation."

"I'm sorry about her," I said.

He was silent a moment. "Yes. I'm sorry, too. And more than sorry. They say it was a very unfortunate accident."

"That's what they say."

"You saw her not long before she—fell."

"Yes."

"Did she talk very much, about me?"

"No," she didn't," I said.

"We hadn't much of a family," he said. "Just her and me."

"I understand. When can I see you?"

"Tonight."

"Couldn't you make it—"

"Tonight, Mr. Rivers."

"All right. Where?"

He hesitated a second time. "You know where the big Walgreen's is out Grand Central?"

"Yes."

"There's a small hotel up the block on the next corner. Called The Palms. Know the place?"

"I can find it."

"Come there. At eight o'clock. Ask the clerk to ring Mr. Southers' room."

"I got it," I said.

The line went dead. I hung up slowly. I stood beside the phone thinking.

The thoughts all added up to the same thing.

There wasn't a move I could make, nothing I could do. Except wait until eight o'clock tonight.

I cruised slowly by the big super drugstore. Its parking area was crowded. Carefree shoppers made an early night rush hour in the drugstore.

Bright street lights, traffic blaring in a night that was even more oppressive with heat than the day just finished. Up ahead a neon winking off and on in the outlines of a palm tree.

I parked the rented car at the curb in front of the hotel.

It was a small, modernistic place. Rawhide and rattan furniture in the lobby. A smart cocktail lounge to one side. A couple came through the swinging doors of the lounge, letting into the lobby the soft sound of laughter and the muted music of a jazz combo.

A dark young man, very neat in a white suit, was at the desk.

I moved over to the desk. The squirt looked up, and I said, "I've got an appointment with Mr. Southers. Will you ring his room?"

"Mr. Southers isn't here."

I glanced at my watch, at the clock on the wall behind the desk.

Western Union and I couldn't both be wrong. It was eight o'clock.

"I'll wait," I said.

"It might prove dreary," the clerk said. "Mr. Southers checked out for good an hour ago."

"Alone?"

"Really, I don't discuss—"

"Okay," I said, "did he leave a message for me? The name is Rivers."

"I'm afraid he didn't."

I turned and walked out.

I sat in the rented car for a few minutes, my fingers tapping the steering wheel.

Then I started the car, turned left at the next intersection, and drove to the Estates.

I parked half a block away, got out of the car and walked to Evie Grove's cottage.

The cozy, low-built, stucco house was dark. I strolled on a few paces, stopped and put my foot on a fire plug to tie my shoe.

My right side screamed bloody murder as I bent over the shoe.

When I straightened, I knew the street was all right for a few seconds. Until a car happened into an intersection, or somebody came out of a nearby house.

I moved quickly up the walk, around the cottage. Near the rear, a room projected so that the outer walls formed a nice dark place.

I slipped the knife from the sheath behind my neck and cut the screen over a window. I'd figured this sort of house would have casement windows rather than the old sash variety.

I was right, and that made the job harder.

I turned the knife around and hit the butt end of it straight against the glass in a short, hard blow. The glass popped softly. It fell inside without a tinkle. There were too many deep rugs in the house for anything to tinkle much. Except her laughter, at the the right times.

I put a couple of fingers through the hole. I could just touch the small brass crank. With pressure against the crank, I managed to push and pull it a few turns. The window swung inward without noise.

I paused to wipe some sweat from my face and let my feeling reach out and touch the neighborhood. Down the street, a bunch of laughing people came out of a house. They sounded as if they were off to a party. Diagonally across the street, an earnest youngster started practicing scales on a piano.

The neighborhood seemed fine.

I undid the screen latch and swung the screen up. Getting through the window required a few minutes. The pain in my side caught me, and I had to take it by inches.

I rested on the plush carpet for a few seconds. Then I got to my feet and moved quietly through the house. Nobody home.

I opened venetian blinds and swung drapes back. My eyes were accustomed to the darkness, and enough light filtered in from outside for me to see what I was doing.

I started the search in the bedroom. The dressing table was bare. No perfume, no cosmetics.

I turned to the closet. It held only a couple of dresses, a suit too heavy for this season, and a pair of discarded sandals.

She would have had luggage. But none was in the closet. None in the entire house.

Evie had packed a couple of bags and gone.

I stood in the darkened living room wiping sweat off my neck.

I stuck the handkerchief in my hip pocket and turned to the phone stand. I picked up the phone book, carried it to the window, and held it against the faint light.

Evie, I figured, was the type to jot phone numbers and addresses on a phone book.

I was wrong.

I dropped the book on the phone stand, opened the drawer.

There was a small white scratch pad inside. I carried the pad to the window and saw that she had jotted an address down.

I didn't need to tear the address off. I'd never had any personal dealings with it, but I knew the address. It was the most expensive place in town.

I wiggled back through the window, dropped to the ground outside, moved to the sidewalk and strolled casually to the rented car.

I wheeled out of the Estates just under the speed limit.

I had the sinking feeling that I was going to miss him, couldn't get to him.

I was keyed tight, with just one thought in mind, and when you are in that condition, you sometimes experience what some people call luck.

There was a light in the old loft building in Ybor City. It flashed off just minutes after I parked the rented car.

I was on the sidewalk, waiting for him to step out of the building. The hot, heavy syrup of sweat crawled down my armpits.

A tall, vulture-faced man stepped out first. Then the shorter man, the one with the chubby, pleasant dark face. The usual cigar was stuck in the moonlike kisser.

I jabbed him in the kidney with the .38.

"Quinton," I said, "you don't want your liver spilled in that gutter."

He stopped, tense, but without fear. The tall man wheeled and stood in that awkward, half-turned position.

"Tell him to get lost," I said.

The chubby face puffed on the cigar. "You realize what you're doing, Rivers?"

"I think so. Tell the goon to go see if he can jump the Hillsborough River."

"Go to hell," Quinton said.

The goon stood teetering on that knife edge.

"Okay," I said, unable to get my voice much further than my throat, "I never thought I'd see the day I'd have to kill just to show that I can."

Quinton hadn't got where he was by lack of nerve. But he knew that I didn't know how to back out.

"Easy," he said quietly and suddenly. He nodded at the tall guy. "Go have a beer."

The tall guy turned and walked away.

"You haven't leveled with me, Quinton," I said.

"No?"

"No. City Hall pressure?"

"I have to watch my step," he said.

"All I wanted was Giles Newell's address. You knew I'd never tag the man who gave it to me."

"What makes you think I got it?"

"I think you know a lot more about Giles and Evie Grove than I do," I said.

"Such as?"

"Get in the car. I can't stand here holding a gun on you all night."

He looked at the coal on his cigar and tossed it away. "That's right. You sure can't."

"Now, Quinton! In the car!"

He slipped a look at me over his shoulder, angled across the sidewalk and got in the car. I shoved him over and got in beside him.

"This climate isn't going to be good for you, Rivers."

"I've never much liked the climate," I said. "And I'm not afraid of you, Quinton. I've never wanted to tangle with you. But I'm not afraid. You carry a grudge, and even City Hall can't help you."

He put another cigar in his face and lighted it.

"How long has Evie Grove worked the ritzy house for you, Quinton?"

"You know I don't have any houses. I'm strictly head of the waiters' and bartenders' association."

"Not the legal association," I said. "But skip that. I'll phrase it another way. How long have you known that Evie Grove was connected with the call spot?"

He sat thinking it over.

He took the cigar out of his mouth and used the thumb of his other hand to pick a fleck of tobacco from his front teeth.

A grin split his face.

"Ed, I don't want to have to fool with a small-timer like you."

"That's fine," I said.

"I could make you plenty of trouble, but I don't see any profit in it."

He looked innocent and bland. I had to remind myself: He keeps close check on all of them. It's part of his business. He would have known about her association with Giles. She couldn't leave town without his knowing.

"I simply don't want you feeling like you scared me into anything, Rivers," he said. "You understand?"

"I think I do."

"I could take care of you," he said, "but I don't see why I should value the risk."

I waited.

"Why don't you," he said, "drive over to Madeira Beach and have a look at 1242 Bayside Boulevard."

CHAPTER

18

FROM TAMPA, take the six-mile bridge across Tampa Bay and you hit St. Petersburg. Go west on Central Avenue for ninety-odd blocks and you reach a beautiful causeway lined with hula-swaying Australian pines. This causeway will get you across Boca Ciega Bay. Boca Ciega Bay and the Gulf of Mexico hug the long fingers of islands, parallel to the mainland and twenty miles or so in length, known to the natives as "The Beaches."

The Gulf side of the beaches is an almost continuous stretch of pure white sand with sighing tropical water breaking in gentle swells and lapping dry rasping foam.

From Pass-A-Grille on the south to the northern end of Indian Rocks, the beaches have divided themselves into endless little independent municipalities. There are probably more city councils and mayors on the beaches than in any comparable area in the country.

There is luxury on the beaches, hundred-thousand-dollar homes and motels so beautiful they seem to have been made by magic from sea froth.

And there is squalor, with shacks and joints squatting on the sand and huddling close.

Madeira had a little of all the elements of the beaches compounded into itself.

I drove past the open-air hot-dog stands, the shacky frame tourist courts crowding against Gulf Boulevard, the bars, seafood places, souvenir stands and bait houses.

I turned off into a filling station just beyond John's Pass, where a channel joins the Gulf and Boca Ciega Bay. I bought some gas and asked the attendant how to find Bayside Boulevard.

He'd never heard of the street, and while he was asking another man at the grease rack, I bought a ready-made sandwich wrapped in wax paper from a vending machine and an icy Coke from a second machine.

As I ate my dinner, the attendant told me how to find the street. It was less than a dozen blocks away, on the bay side of the island. A new street in a new development that had been recently pumped up out of the bay.

A few minutes later I was driving down Bayside. There were long stretches of new fill. The land looked powdery and uncured. Here and there were houses and private docks in various stages of construction. The several newly completed houses looked nice—pastel stuccos and glass.

Most of the houses had numbers plainly visible. I got out of the car three times to see a number.

There was no 1242.

I sat in the car, thinking of Quinton and feeling a metallic edge come to my teeth.

Half a mile ahead, a lighted cabin cruiser was coming up the bay. The lights disappeared briefly, then reappeared.

It took me a few seconds to realize that a building down on the point had cut the lights from view.

I started the car and drove down there. A low, sprawling cottage was on the end of the fill just before the road made its circular turn-around.

I cut the ignition and lights, got out of the car and walked to the cottage.

There was a metal number plate keeping company with the sparse grass sprigs and bedraggled, newly set baby palms.

1242.

I put my hand in the pocket that held the .38 and moved up the walk to the front door. I put my finger on the buzzer button. I could hear the buzzer skirling inside, but no other sounds came from the dark house.

The cruiser had gone on up the bay and the nearest house was a half-mile away. Across the lagoon formed by the land fill the lights of Madeira Beach twinkled. But they were a mile away.

I tried the door. It was locked.

I made a circuit of the house. All the windows were locked.

In this weather.

There was a three-year-old convertible in the carport adjoining the house.

I went back to the front door.

There are good developers in Florida and bad ones. This one had cut a few corners. I wedged the tip of the knife blade past the door molding and sprung the spring-type lock.

Inside, the house was stifling. I heard the low hum of a refrigerator clicking on, the sound of a heavy flying insect throwing itself against the window that showed the lights a mile away.

I guessed from the indistinct outlines of furniture that I was in a living room. Attached would be a glassed-in Florida room. A little hall would lead off the living room to a couple of bedrooms and a connecting bath. The refrigerator hum told of a compact kitchenette to my left.

I moved forward a few steps.

My foot struck a yielding mass.

I stepped back.

I didn't want any light right away.

I wiped my forehead with the back of my hand, reached in my pocket and got out a paper book of matches. They were damp and contrary. I mashed one up; then I got one to light.

The pale glow fell across her face. The blond hair flowed out from her scalp to make a golden fan on the carpet. Gone were the vague dreams, the fear of someday finding herself without money, the disorganized morality.

Evie had been shot under the left breast. I knew the bullet had struck her heart, for she hadn't bled much.

The man lay a dozen feet beyond her. He had been shot in the temple, and he hadn't bled much either.

He had fallen so that he lay on his side with his left arm stuffed under him and his right arm a little outflung, crooked at the elbow.

The match flared out and I lit another.

He was a tall, wide-shouldered, athletic-looking man. His face was squarish, rugged, masculine. He had been good looking, and it hadn't got him that rich wife after all.

Just to make sure, I pulled a wallet out of his pocket. The driver's license was made out to Giles Newell.

. I put the wallet back in his pocket and turned his body. His other pocket yielded only some keys and change.

But the gun was revealed. He had fallen on it.

The match scorched my fingers. I blew it out. Hunkered beside Giles, I put it together. Giles's sister, the Hofstetter woman, had known the score. Crowded, she'd got scared—and written off. This had caused Giles to decide the water was too deep. The promise of more easy money than he'd ever heard of, or direct force, had lured him from his appointment with me. He'd let Evie know where he was and she'd turned up.

Now it was all wrapped up, closed for all time. The picture was here for the cops. Doors and windows locked from the inside. A lovers' quarrel. Man shoots woman, then himself. It happens often enough not to be unique.

And a great silence covers forever whatever it was that Giles Newell knew.

It could have been that way.

Tulman could be guilty.

Mrs. Hofstetter might have fallen.

Giles could have committed murder and suicide.

Each thing a separate event from every other.

It could have been that simple. And I wished it was, as a dark, haunting picture of beauty took form in my mind. I remembered the way she moved as she walked, how she'd looked on the beach with the storm breaking over us.

I remembered, and I wished. And I thought: How easy. Just walk out. Let the spring lock fasten the door as the last person out of here let it.

I stood up with the gun in my hand. I knew it would carry only one set of prints, Newell's.

I wiped the gun, carried it to the far side of the room, and dropped it on the carpet.

It was double murder now.

With my handkerchief, I wiped everything in the room I'd touched. I set the snap on the spring lock, stepped outside, and closed the door with the handkerchief between my hand and the doorknob.

I turned away from the unlocked door, walked back to the car and got in.

I swung the car in the circular turn-around, gave it the gas.

I didn't look back.

CHAPTER

19

I DROVE back to Tampa. I knew I hadn't much time. I had to be right. Quinton could reveal that I'd had the Madeira Beach address. The service-station attendant would peg me as the man who'd asked directions to Bayside Boulevard. Julian Patrick could depict me as a sometime violent man who'd hunted hard for Giles Newell.

I dodged through Tampa traffic out to the Estates. I parked the car at the curbing, crossed the street and went up the walk to Laura's house.

She answered my ring quickly. I moved inside and closed the door.

She laid her hand on my arm and led me to the couch. "You look very tired, Ed."

I nodded.

She asked, "Would you like something to eat?"

"A sandwich, a cold beer."

"I'll bring it to you," she said.

She went to the kitchen. I sank down on the couch. She came back with a tray of sandwiches, a carafe of coffee and an icy-beaded open bottle of beer. She put the tray on the cocktail table in front of the couch.

I picked up a sandwich. "I want you to go away for a few days."

She raised her eyes in a question.

"It's just a safety measure," I said.

"Safety measure?"

"I saw Giles Newell tonight."

"Did he—"

"He was dead. Along with his woman friend."

I saw the shock hit her. She swayed a little. I put my sandwich down and took her hands in mine.

"Then we've failed, Ed Rivers," she said.

"Not yet. It was made to look like murder and suicide. It doesn't look that way now. I tampered a little with the scene of the crime."

Her large, dark eyes looked into mine. "The person you're after will surmise you're behind it. Is that what you're saying?"

"Something like that."

"This will arouse desperation in that person."

"I wouldn't be surprised."

"And you don't want me near you."

"I guess I'm a little dangerous," I said, "like a walking time bomb."

"Where could I go, Ed?"

"Take a trip."

She withdrew her hands. They lay in her lap. She sat looking at them.

"In some ways," she said, "you're like Wally."

"I am?"

"Oh, you're poles apart, but you have decency and consideration. He wanted me to take a trip too, during and after the trial."

"Why didn't you?"

"I don't know. Honestly, I don't. Most of the women I

know would have traveled a long way from the scandal and pain. I guess I just felt it wouldn't be right." She raised her eyes. "I'm sorry I got you into this, Ed."

"You didn't," I said. "You tried, but I wasn't in it until somebody tried to knock my brains out. You could say I was pitched into it by the scalp."

"If I'd left you alone—"

"You couldn't have, for you were fighting for him. I'm glad I'm in it. I've found something I lost a long time ago —somebody I can believe in."

She forced a grin. "Maybe you don't know me well enough, Ed."

"I know you're a lady. I know you live by a code. That's enough."

"You idealistic roughneck. Your beer's getting warm."

The food and drink gave me back some strength. We didn't say anything more as I finished eating.

The door buzzer sounded.

Laura started to get up, but remained seated as I made a motion with my hand. I moved along the wall to the window beside the front door. I cracked the edge of the drape and looked out.

The buzzer demanded attention.

A black car was parked at the curb in front of the house.

I backed along the wall until I reached the opening giving to the hallway. I pointed at myself and shook my head. Then I pointed at Laura and swung my hand in the direction of the front door. As she nodded, I jabbed my finger toward the empty beer bottle, glass, and plates on the cocktail table.

She picked the things up quickly and carried them to the kitchen.

As the buzzer gave a third long, insistent peal, she called, "Just a moment. I'm coming."

She walked across the living area, passing by me as I stood in the dark hall well. She didn't look at me.

I heard the carpet-muffled touch of her feet come to a halt. I sensed the noiseless opening of the front door.

I heard Julian Patrick say, "Good evening, Mrs. Tulman."

"How do you do, Lieutenant," she said coolly. "Aren't you working late?"

"Servant of the people," Julie said, irony in his voice. "May I come in?"

"So this is a business call."

"I'm afraid it is."

"Well," Laura said, "I wasn't expecting a social call. Yes, you may come in."

I heard the soft sound of feet, the click of the front door as it closed. I faded a few steps back in the hallway.

"Won't you sit down, Lieutenant?"

"Thank you." Julie sighed as he sat.

"I think we can dispense with all the niceties, Lieutenant," Laura said. "Just what's on your mind?"

"I'm looking for Ed Rivers."

"Has something come up?"

"Something has. Have you seen him?"

"I've seen quite a bit of him in the past few days."

"Have you seen him in the last hour?"

"What makes you think I might have?"

"You're his client."

"That's no reason he should call here at this hour of the evening."

Julie was silent. I knew he was studying every flicker of expression on her face, in her eyes.

I sensed what was coming. *Don't look toward the hall entry, Laura!*

"I think he might have had reason to call here," Julie said.

"Really."

"You haven't answered my question."

"I've been quite alone the last hour, Lieutenant."

Again he was silent. Then he said very quietly, "I don't believe you, Mrs. Tulman."

"That's your privilege."

"We don't want to see you in trouble, Mrs. Tulman."

"I appreciate that."

"But we do want to know what Rivers told you."

"He told me nothing. I haven't seen him. Was his car outside?"

"Not at the house."

"Any sign of him in here?"

"Not in this room, Mrs. Tulman."

"What do you mean by that?"

"There are several rooms in this house."

"You think I might be hiding him?"

"I think the idea of getting your husband off has become an obsession. I think you might try to help Rivers for that reason."

"I've told you—he hasn't been here."

"Mrs. Tulman," Julie chided, "there *is* a car. Not here. It's parked across the street. A rental car. I know that Ed uses rental cars or cabs when he's on a case."

"Anyone can rent a car, Lieutenant. A rental car in the neighborhood doesn't prove anything."

"But it asks for proof," Julie said.

"Why should I lie to you?"

"Because Rivers lied to you."

"About what?"

"About Madeira Beach."

"I'm afraid this is all a riddle to me, Lieutenant."

"I think not," he said, steel creeping into his voice. "Two people were killed on Madeira Beach tonight."

"How shocking!"

"Murdered."

She didn't answer that."

"Giles Newell was one of them, Mrs. Tulman," Julie said,

his voice holding an insistent ring. "Rivers was going to any length to find him."

"To make him tell the truth, Lieutenant!"

"To make him talk," Julie said. "I'll agree with you that far. Truth, falsehood. It wouldn't matter to Ed. He was out to make Newell say what he wanted Newell to say."

"I don't believe that."

"I don't care what you believe, Mrs. Tulman," Julie said, now insultingly polite.

He was reaching a moment of decision, whether or not I'd spotted his arrival in time to get away from the house.

"We know," Julie said, "that Rivers went to Madeira Beach tonight."

"How do you know?"

"A phoned tip, Mrs. Tulman."

Quinton. From Quinton, I thought.

"We know further," Patrick continued, "that Rivers arrived in Madeira and asked directions to Bayside Boulevard, where the double murder took place."

I faded back in the hallway, wondering which way his decision would fall. I slid around a door jamb into a bedroom. A big, spacious bedroom. Maybe it was hers.

As I turned to press against the wall, I wondered if the window and screen could be opened noiselessly. I looked at the window.

I saw a face there.

The small, white moon of a face.

I caught my breath. Before I could move, the face was gone. I crossed to the window, but I couldn't see or hear him. The lawn muffled the quick scamper of his feet, and the night had swallowed him.

20

I COULDN'T RISK the screen. It was copper, mounted on an aluminum frame. The frame was set with thumb screws. The screen would either have to be cut or lifted out bodily. Either way, Patrick would hear me.

It was a long, bad period of time. I stayed close to the wall, the .38 in my hand. I knew the possible results, but if he decided to search the house, forcing his way without a warrant, I'd have slugged him.

His brittle voice continued to question her. For all his arrogance and quality of mercilessness, Patrick wore his mental dancing shoes when confronted with wealth and power. He didn't treat Laura as he would have treated a washwoman from Ybor City, or Evie Grove, or a Franklin Street dime-store clerk accused of stealing.

At last Laura said, "All right, Lieutenant, he was here."

"When?"

"For half an hour or so before you arrived. He was nervous. He kept watching out the front. He saw your car and went out the back way."

"What am I to believe?" Patrick said.

"Whatever you like," Laura said. Her voice held a careless, don't-care ring that gave it sincerity. "I've kept you talking, Lieutenant, to give him a chance to get away."

"That's tampering with the law."

"You wish to arrest me?"

"Not until I get my hands on Rivers."

"Good evening, Lieutenant."

I heard the sounds of his departure. I moved to the hall archway, staying in the shadows of the hall.

"Don't look this way, Laura," I said.

She was standing a few feet away in the living area. She looked straight ahead.

I heard Patrick's car start outside and move off.

"He's gone," Laura said.

"No, he's just waiting."

I could see the clean, classic profile of her face. A faint quiver came to her chin. "Ed . . . you didn't . . . there's no truth in Patrick's accusations?"

"Do you think so?"

"No. I had to ask, that's all. He voiced the question. I couldn't help but ask. But don't answer. It wouldn't show much faith on my part if you had to answer."

I looked from the darkness into the light at her. I said, "I'm going to pitch the key to the rented car onto the couch. Sit down. Pick up the key. Stay there a moment. Then get up, go outside, drive the car to the Ajax agency and catch a cab home."

"Will do, Ed."

"He'll follow you. You won't see him, but he'll be back there. Until you leave the car at the agency. He'll decide then that I did get out of the house. He'll throw out a city-wide dragnet."

"Ed—"

"Don't talk. We haven't any time left."

She hugged her arms together for a second.

"Here comes the key," I said. "If I miss the couch, watch the way you pick the key up."

The key was on a short chain attached to an ID tag. I pitched it low and pretty hard. It glinted for a second before it struck the back rest of the couch. It lay almost in the center of the couch.

She moved to the couch easily, sat down and rested her head against the back of the couch for a moment. She looked like a woman gaining a seed of strength to combat weariness for a little longer.

When she got up, she had the key in her hand. She walked to a long, low blond table against the wall of the room, picked up a purse.

Without looking in my direction, she walked toward the front door. She was out of my line of vision now. I heard the door open and close.

I followed her in my mind. She was outside, trying the door. She would move quickly down the walk, up the sidewalk. A glance around before she crossed the street.

Patrick would be giving orders to the flunky driving the black, unmarked car now.

She was walking calmly and swiftly, angling across the street.

Opening the rented car. It would take her another minute to locate the ignition switch and unfamiliar gear, gas and brake controls.

She had the car in motion. Half a block. A block.

Patrick wouldn't let her get too far before the black car was in motion also.

I stood waiting, giving them time. Not thinking of what would happen if the guess was wrong, if Patrick pegged her as a decoy. If the black car didn't leave the neighborhood.

I went out of the house by the back way. In the patio I paused. I looked at the spot where the little girl's body had been found.

Then I went around the back corner of the house. To the window looking into Laura's bedroom.

I didn't find any tracks.

But I was the only one who knew definitely that no tracks were there.

I turned and crossed the wide back lawn. I reached the

edge of the Collins property. I could hear water lapping softly against the seawall. I passed the private dock where the Collins cruiser bobbed, a sleek creature of the sea chaffing at its moorings.

There were soft lights in the Collins house. I approached over the long stretch of lawn from the back of the house, the patio side. I could make out a cool white wrought-iron-and-glass table and chairs, a barbecue pit, a gaily colored beach umbrella like a canopy over the little-used outdoor facilities.

I went around the house, eased to the front door. The place was very quiet.

I pressed my thumb on the buzzer. I heard it sing. Then Milt Collins opened the front door. He didn't look good. His hair was tangled. His face was pale, filled with a shadow that gave it a gaunt cast. His eyes were red and sunken into their sockets. He was dressed in slacks and a sport shirt unbuttoned halfway down his chest.

He was a man at war with himself. A man needing a big, stiff drink desperately, and just as desperately needing not to take it.

He looked at me almost dumbly.

"Can I come in?" I asked.

"No. What do you want?"

"I want your help," I said.

"I can't help you. Go away. Stay away, Rivers."

"You're the only one who can help me," I said. "Did you know that?"

"No."

"You'll have to help me. You can't avoid it," I said.

"The hell I can't! Get out of here," he said.

He started to close the door. I wedged my shoulder against it.

"Giles Newell is dead," I said.

"What?" His jaw sagged.

"And Evie Grove."

"No—no! You're lying!"

"I wish I were," I said.

"How?"

"Both of them were murdered," I said. "Tonight."

I pushed against the door. He let it yield. I stepped into the living area of the house. He stood looking at me stupidly, his arms hanging.

From the next room came the voice of old lady Wherry. "Who is it, Milt?"

"Rivers."

She came into the room. Max the Giant drifted in behind her.

"What are you doing here?" she demanded, fixing a cold pair of eyes on me.

"Trying to stay on my feet, Mrs. Wherry. I was asking Milt to help me."

"You're no more concern of ours, Mr. Rivers. I appreciate your getting the pictures back. They've been destroyed. If you want more money, I'm afraid you're out of luck."

"I'm not asking for money, Mrs. Wherry. I'm simply asking for Milt's help."

"You shan't bother us again, Mr. Rivers. Now leave. Or I'll call the police. We are preparing to take a trip. Get away from all this. It seems there's no end to it."

Like a destroyer moving to protect a convoy, she crossed the room to the phone.

I watched her without saying anything. Until her hand was on the phone.

"I'm not going to stop you," I said. "Go right ahead. I'll show them what I have."

The enduring pride and tirelessness of her blunt, old face changed to anger. "Mr. Rivers, we are not in the least interested—"

She broke off as the remaining member of the family came into the room. Young Bryan looked at us all, coolly, calmly, with a detachment not belonging to a thirteen-year-old boy.

"Is anything wrong, Father?" he inquired.

"Bryan," his grandmother said, "it's past your bedtime."

He looked at her as he might regard a not very interesting specimen of bug under a microscope. It brought suffering to the old lady's eyes.

He shrugged and went into the den. In a moment, the sound of a television quiz show filtered into the room from the den.

I looked at Milt Collins and said, "His footprints are under Mrs. Tulman's window."

Milt said nothing. His head drooped a trifle. I could feel it in him. A great darkness, like a death wish.

"You see," I said, "you really must help me. The easiest way would have been the honest way in the beginning."

"Mr. Rivers!" Mrs. Wherry barked.

"Shut up," Milt told her softly. "You know everything, don't you, Rivers?"

"Yes," I said.

"How much can you prove?"

"Enough to get them started. The local police. The D.A.'s office. The state men. Once they know the direction to look, they'll find proof plenty, and that's for sure."

He passed his fingers through his hair. He dropped his hand and looked at it. Then he half-raised both hands and looked at them together. Big, strong, worker's hands. The hands of a leader.

Honest hands, once upon a time.

"I guess it's been for sure always," he said, and I knew he was talking about many things.

He lowered his hands and looked at me. "Can you understand, Rivers?"

"Yes—they were your children."

"And Stephanie's," he said.

He seemed blind for a moment. Then he asked, "Can it be handled quietly?"

"I'm afraid not. I'll try—but I can't make promises."

He shivered and pulled in his shoulders. "It will certainly provide a bloody Roman holiday. At our expense. Us. It's happening to us."

"You can't undo it," I said.

"No—and it was such a lousy party that night. They were all lousy to me. That was one that stunk, even to Stephanie. We were there, while our kids—"

"Milt," Mrs. Wherry said in a hoarse whisper, "I forbid you to say another word."

He looked at her blankly. "You should never have mothered a daughter by him, Mama Wherry. You should have known."

"Milt—"

"Old Spicola Wherry. Great lover of freaks. Fine old citizen of Tampa. A freak himself. Only it didn't show on the outside. Worst kind of freak. Finding in the company of freaks the only people with whom he could feel at home. It shimmered close to the surface with Stephanie. It grew to full blossom inside of Bryan."

The old lady seemed to choke. Milt looked at her with a great weariness. Max the Giant looked at her and shared the suffering in the old lady's eyes.

Milt dragged his gaze to mine. "What made you so sure, Rivers?"

"Newell's death," I said. "It meant he had lied at Tulman's trial. If the time element was wrong, the little girl could not have been killed on the Tulman patio. No one was there to kill her. She had been killed someplace else and carried there.

"Then I began to think of a strange little boy. A little boy who never plays, who has no friends, who can view the drunkenness of a father and the insanity of a mother with an absolute lack of feeling. It all added up to a little boy who got born with some pieces missing, who would put ammonia in a goldfish bowl to watch the reaction and then describe it as his sister's doing. A little boy who was such a terror in small, weird ways that you couldn't keep a house servant. Or do I have to go to the employment agencies, run down servants and get statements as to why they quit?"

"Why bother them?" Milt asked. "Go ahead, Rivers, tell me about my kid." Behind his eyes, he was writhing in agony.

"A little boy," I said, "living in a world peopled by a population of one. Yet his physical development proceeds at a normal pace.

"In the company of this boy put a girl nearly his own age. In his world there are strange conceptions—and no conceptions. No conception of right and wrong, of her as a sister, of civilized conduct, or morals—"

"Stop!" the old lady said. She moved toward me, not with the power and certainty that had been hers. She hobbled. "We are very rich, Mr. Rivers. No price is too high. We'll give you anything."

"I wish I could take it," I said. "But the only price I can take is a statement from Milt, to save a man's life. At least, we could save one life out of all this."

"No," said Mrs. Wherry. "I'll not have it!"

"Yes," Milt said. He moved to a blond desk, sat down, got a piece of paper from a drawer and started writing.

The ball-point pen he used glided without a sound.

"It should be you, Mrs. Wherry, writing the statement," I said. "You—in one part of this house while the tragedy began in another. You, determined to keep this house from being engulfed by its foundations of disease and sand. Carrying the body of the child away. Not knowing then what else you could do. Improvising. Determined to fight in every way you could.

"You knew when Wallace Tulman returned. You called

the Yacht Club, talked to Newell, found Tulman had been drinking alone, that no one could say for sure what time he had left.

"The formless desperation in you began to shape into a plan. You knew Giles Newell could be bought. You would sacrifice Tulman. Only Tulman. Then it would all be over.

"But it wasn't over. And you had to keep making the blood sacrifices to the idol of family pride you'd set up. First the Hofstetter woman. Then because her death scared her brother, Giles, you had to lure him from talking to me with an offer of untold wealth. Lure him to death, because you knew the remnants of the family would never be safe so long as he lived.

"You had a very efficient extension of yourself—Max the Giant. To slug me, try to scare me off, to run me down with a car."

She looked at the mountainous mass of muscle and sinew with the pink seal's head. "He never killed anyone, Rivers. I ask for nothing to be done that I cannot do myself. I went to the Hofstetter woman when she made her demands. I went to the Madeira Beach cottage with a gun. I'm very sorry Evie Grove walked into the picture."

The pink seal's head swung slowly back and forth on the massive shoulders. There were tears in his eyes. "Mrs. Wherry—"

"I'm sorry, Max. I fear Mr. Rivers is right. There is no end to the course I tried to chart. There is only one possible end."

She watched Milt drop the ball-point pen on the desk. She watched me cross to the desk and pick up the written statement.

Then she called gently, "Bryan . . ."

He came out of the den. "Yes, Grandmère?"

"Come to me, child."

He walked to her. She reached and took his hand. "We must take a short trip, Bryan."

"Must we, Grandmère?"

"Yes. Max will see that we're not disturbed."

The generations of the Wherry family walked out of the room quickly.

Milt raised his head. Then he leaped to his feet. Max hit him flush on the chin and Milt was out cold.

I realized what was happening then.

I tried to dodge around Max. He threw a hard blow at my face. It caught me on the cheek and knocked me down. The giant was invincible.

He aimed a kick at my stomach. I rolled away, gained my feet. I was trying to pull the .38 when he closed in on me. I lost the gun as we wrestled backward.

We fell over a coffee table. In falling, I twisted sideways. His grip broke and I was free of him.

I scrabbled toward the door.

I thought of the cruiser bobbing at the dock, and of the great, dark reaches of Tampa Bay, and of an old lady and a little boy marching to the cruiser.

Max the Giant grabbed my leg and dragged me down.

CHAPTER

21

THE WILD SWING of his fist ended against my rib cage. I felt as if every bone in my body had been broken. I jabbed his eyeballs with my thumbs and fought him back for a moment. I had to rise above the agony in my side.

While I had him off balance, I kicked him in the groin. As he tried to bring my neck into the crook of his elbow, I clamped my teeth into the flesh of his forearm. I heard the grinding of my teeth as they met.

He bleated softly with pain and rolled away. I was on my feet again.

He half-circled me, placing himself between me and the door.

His arms were hooked wide as he came in. His arms swept up. He threw a judo chop at the side of my neck, but he'd used that one on me before. I sidestepped that one and ducked the one that followed.

My hand went to the back of my neck and came down holding the knife.

He snatched at the knife. The edge of the blade wiped crimson across his palm.

"Stay back," I said. "I don't want to use it."

The pink seal's head moved back and forth. The great arms reached. I went back, but not fast enough. His arms closed on me.

We reeled and fell.

I felt the knife strike yielding substance.

I saw the light go out of his eyes. It flared high, briefly, a light of bewilderment and pain.

Then it was turned off forever.

I rolled away from him. Took hold of a chair. Pulled myself upright.

My knees were trembling. They wouldn't hold me for a moment, and I had to stand holding to the chair.

Sweat rose about me like a thick, gagging steam. I took a step from the chair, another.

I was outside and moving toward the dock.

I couldn't see their shadows. Then I heard the whir of the electric starter.

I forced myself to a run. The motor of the cruiser barked to life and settled to a soft run.

The boat moved away. I fell to my knees on the dock and watched it go.

The shadow of the boat receded rapidly, until there was no shadow left. Only the sound of the motor fading into the darkness.

Then the sound finally stopped altogether. The bay was very quiet. Even the pale, moonlit clouds seemed to have stopped their motion in the sky.

I heard the faint echoes of the splash. Carried a long way across the water.

Then the second splash.

And I knew I would hear nothing else out there.

I got to my feet and stumbled from the dock. I looked at the Collins house and wondered if he would ever have the strength to rise above all this.

I looked at the Tulman house and felt the pull of it carrying me in that direction.

Inside, I made my way to the living area and sank in a vast and comfortable chair. I sat there pulling breath in and out of my lungs. For a moment I wanted only stillness.

Finally, I stirred. I pulled Milt Collins' statement from my pocket. It was wrinkled and damp with my sweat.

I sat holding it. Holding Tulman's life in my hands. Wondering, if I could turn back the clock, if I would do it over again.

I knew that I would. And I knew it would turn out exactly this way.

Tulman would never know the animal vigor of her, for he could never arouse it.

But I would never know it, either. Except to know it was there. For I would never have her.

I knew that now. With this house around me—and my apartment on the edges of Ybor City waiting for me.

I knew it with the memory of her lips and the storm over us.

I knew it with the knowledge that I had aroused an elemental something that no other man would ever bring to
life in her.

But Tulman possessed the civilized part of her, and in
her that was the strongest part.

I heard a taxi stop outside. I uncoiled out of the chair,
and when she walked in, I handed her Milt's statement. I
handed her back to her husband. And compared to this,
everything else had been a breeze.

For this was the hardest thing I'd ever done.